Rio Connection

by

Carol Henry

This is a work of fiction. Names, characters, places, and incidents are either the product of the author's imagination or are used fictitiously, and any resemblance to actual persons living or dead, business establishments, events, or locales, is entirely coincidental.

Rio Connection

COPYRIGHT © 2014 by Carol Henry

Cover Art by *RJ Morris*

The Wild Rose Press, Inc.
PO Box 708
Adams Basin, NY 14410-0708
Visit us at www.thewildrosepress.com

Publishing History
First Crimson Rose Edition, 2014
Print ISBN 978-1-62830-409-1
Digital ISBN 978-1-62830-410-7

Published in the United States of America

Marcia dropped the flimsy garment as if it burned her hands. It floated to the floor. Embarrassment warmed her cheeks. She lowered her head, not wanting Jared to see how flustered she was over being caught with such sexy items in her hand. She stepped to the side of the bed and looked around the room. She hadn't unpacked her toiletries, but like the other contents in her luggage, they were haphazardly strewn everywhere.

What did they think she was hiding? What were they looking for? What had Russell gotten himself into?

"Are you sure?" Jared exclaimed to whoever was on the other end of the phone.

She faced him and found puzzled eyes—and that sexy raised eyebrow staring back at her. "Kline. The last name is Kline. Marcia Kline."

"Holcomb," she stated, heat flooding her face for the second time in a matter of minutes. He raised the other eyebrow.

"Holcomb," he said into the mouthpiece, never taking his eyes off her. "Yes, room 1036. Bradley Holcomb?"

She nodded to confirm his question and settled in the chair next to the window. She gazed out at the moonlight, not wanting to see the shock on his face.

He hung up the phone and sank into the chair opposite her. "If you're married, where's Mr. Holcomb?"

"If you must know, I have no idea."

"Is he with you here in Rio?"

"No. He's back in New York. We're not married."

Damn! Now he was aware of what a pathetic loser she really was—going on a honeymoon without the groom.

Praise for Carol Henry's stories

NOTHING SHORT OF A MIRACLE
"Carol Henry is a gifted writer who paints you a picture of all the fine details of the season. A master at pacing…the ins and outs of the developing romance are a delight to read…The story is like a warm hug."

~ *W. A. Darling*
25 Days of Christmas Stories Review
~*~

AMAZON CONNECTION
"…a fast paced suspense that will have you reading as fast as possible to get to the next page. The description of the Amazon jungle will make you feel like you are actually there."

~*You Gotta Read Reviews*
~*~

SHANGHAI CONNECTION
Voted #2 Best Book/E-Book Romance Novel
2012 Preditors & Editors Reader's Poll
~*~

"Carol Henry's beautifully written descriptions immerse you in the surroundings where there are plenty of edge-of-the-seat thrills…a connection you want to make!"

~*Mal Olson,*
author of adrenaline kicked romantic suspense
~*~

"Rich with setting and suspense…Carol Henry brings the setting alive with lush, vivid descriptions…and keeps you turning pages until the very end."

~*Alicia Dean, romantic suspense author*

Dedication

To my husband, Gary,
my high school sweetheart, and my travel buddy—
here's to another great adventure.

Acknowledgments

Special thanks to my granddaughter, Reneé Smith, for her help with the hospital/I.C.U. medical information; to my dear friend, Thea McGinnis, for her creative "on the spot" input; and to my sister, Stephanie, for taking the time to read and give feedback on *Rio Connection.*

And to a fabulous editor, Ally Robertson, thanks for your support and friendship.

Prologue

Russell Kline sat at the crowded outdoor café next to the hotel across from Copacabana Beach. The large red awning overhead kept the hot Brazilian sun off his already sunburned head. The lively music blaring over the loudspeakers irritated, making his conversation with Ricardo and Paul almost impossible without having to shout. He leaned his elbows on the table, drawing closer to the two men. The Brazilians did the same.

"When can I meet your marketing rep?" He swiped the napkin over his sweaty forehead, all the while not losing eye contact.

"Why is Mr. Rose not meeting us? Why has he sent you?" Paul linked his fingers together on top of the table and angled his head sideways.

Russell detected the mistrust in Paul's creased eyebrows—the cold, calculating, sinister man he'd hoped to avoid.

"Mr. Rose was unable to get away. He is on another assignment for the company. He asked me to come in his place."

"Do you have the avatar prototype?" Ricardo nudged his partner, but kept his eyes on Russell.

Unlike his partner, Ricardo was shorter, pudgier, and wore a happy face as if he was in his glory dealing with the underworld of secrecy.

"Yes. I was assured your Mr. Osaka was ready for

the latest release. I came to make sure there are no screw-ups this time."

"Yes, yes," Ricardo confirmed, shifting in his chair. "You will meet Mr. Osaka soon. He has instructed us to inform you to meet him on the beach where no one will overhear your conversation, or see the exchange. You understand. Yes?"

"I assume you refer to this beach across the street. It's a long beach. Exactly where am I to meet him?"

"Yes, a location further down Copacabana Beach. But first we must be assured you have the prototype. Can you show it to us now?"

The man hedged, not divulging the location. Russell held his tongue, playing their game.

"Would I be sitting at this table with you if I didn't have the flash drive with me?" He stared at Paul and Ricardo, daring them to prove him wrong.

The two men looked at each other, and then nodded in agreement over their unspoken consensus.

"You are to walk down the beach a couple kilometers. You will see a group of trees," Paul instructed, not taking his eyes off Russell. "Mr. Osaka will meet you there in half an hour. Make sure you have the package."

"I'll have to go back to my room and get it from the safe. It will take longer than thirty minutes to go back to the hotel and then walk so far down the beach. Tell Mr. Osaka I'll be there in an hour or the deal is off."

"We will contact him while we wait at this café for you to return. We will go with you to meet Mr. Osaka."

"I don't need an audience when I meet with Mr. Osaka. I will go on my own. You can stay here if you wish, but I think our meeting is over, gentlemen."

Russell stood, threw a few bills on the table, and walked with ease back to his hotel. Who was this Mr. Rose? There was no one at the company by the name of Rose—not even close. He hoped he hadn't blown his cover. These two bumbling idiots didn't seem smart enough to figure out a bluff when one was right in front of them. If all went well, this would be the last sale of Jared's high-tech interactive avatar games to the Japanese.

Chapter One

Too angry to cry, Marcia Kline drew her powder blue Prius to a stop in her sister's drive and sat for a second to catch her breath and dry her eyes. Talk about being blindsided. She hadn't seen it coming. She was every cliché ever used to describe her current situation—the "last to know" being an accurate one.

She had to talk to someone, and her sister had always been there when she needed a shoulder to cry on. She'd been there when their mother and father had been killed in a car accident, and she'd been there when Geoffrey had walked out on her three years ago. Samantha, an excellent sounding board, was never judgmental, never full of fly-by-night advice. She never said I told you so.

Marcia opened the car door, swung her legs out, and stood in one fluid motion. The cold New York, February air hit her full force. She tugged her scarf tight around her neck to anchor her long hair in place to keep it from flying around her head and whipping across her face. Holding the scarf tight in her hands, she made a mad dash up the shoveled sidewalk, the two steps to the front door, and jabbed at the door bell. Before her sister had a chance to answer, Marcia let herself inside.

"Sammie. It's me," she called out. "Where are you?"

She stomped her feet free of the snow clinging to

her ankle-high boots, then slipped out of them and set them on the boot rack behind the door.

"I'm in the kitchen. Come on in."

Her sister was almost always in the kitchen baking something delicious. Marcia breathed in the tantalizing aroma of fresh banana bread, drawing her through the foyer into the bright kitchen.

"Smells good in here as usual. How much longer before whatever it is, is ready to come out of the oven? Smells like bananas."

"Minutes. Let me put the coffee on."

Her sister had the brew going in record time as if she'd anticipated her visit.

"So, how'd it go? Did you surprise Brad with your basket of hors d'oeuvres today? I can't wait to hear every detail." Samantha wiped her hands on a towel, then sat down at the kitchen table. She rested her chin in her hands, a broad smile on her waiting face, and sighed. "It sounded so romantic…"

"That's what I anticipated. But then I walked in and surprised the dirty rat," Marcia cut her sister short. Her voice cracked, tears formed, she swallowed, and brushed her hair back behind her ears.

Sammie shot back in her seat. "Wait! What happened? That doesn't sound very romantic. You don't sound like someone who is about to marry the man of her dreams."

"Well, I'm not. Marrying him, I mean. How could I when I walked into his office only to find him in the arms of another woman."

Marcia held back a sob, her voice wobbled.

"*What!*" her sister shrieked this time. "Brad? Another woman? Are you sure? Who?"

"I saw them with my own eyes. He was definitely with another woman. They were both naked. I'm pretty sure it was Jessica from our aerobics class," she sniffed. "I didn't stick around to say hi. One thing for sure, I won't be going back to her class. My God, Sammie, what is wrong with me? Why do men keep walking out on me? Cheating on me?"

"To begin with, there is nothing wrong with you. You take care of yourself—you work out at the gym, you're a very caring woman. And you're beautiful without flaunting your good looks. It's the men who can't seem to keep their zippers zipped when they're around young bimbos. I hope you told him to get lost."

Marcia looked at her sister—a shorter image of herself. The wheat blonde hair, wide stark blue eyes, and peaches and cream skin were all family traits she considered ordinary. She dismissed her sister's glowing comments said in an effort to make her feel better.

"Yes, I told him the wedding was off. As far as I'm concerned he can take care of the caterer," she hiccupped, "the florist, the musicians, the reception, and he can return all the gifts."

"Good for you. At least this time you won't be the one left to face the embarrassment of it all."

"I feel like such a fool. I handed in my resignation to Wild and Wonderful a month ago, and they've already hired someone to take my place. I gave up my apartment anticipating moving in with Brad after the wedding, and it's already been leased. Everything is in boxes except for the clothes I packed to take to Rio de Janeiro for our honeymoon."

She covered her face with her hands. Tears fell between her fingers. She lowered her head on folded arms on top of the table in defeat.

Sammie patted and stroked her hair like a small woebegone child—the tender endearment the last straw. A sob escaped. *God, she was pathetic.* She drew in a deep breath and then sat up straight in her chair. She refused to cry another tear over Brad-the-Rat!

She wouldn't.

The coffeemaker beeped. Rich, strong aroma filled the kitchen. Her sister pulled cups from the cabinet and poured two steaming cups of coffee. Placing the cups, cream and sugar on the table, she went to the oven, opened the door, and transferred the steaming banana bread to the cooling rack on the counter. The rich, sweet fragrance blended with the scent of the coffee and softened Marcia's insides. It reminded her of their mother, the warm family gatherings in the kitchen. *This* kitchen that her sister now owned. Sammie was a lot like their mother. Nurturing, caring, and always comforting.

"Look, you know I don't like to give you a whole lot of advice. But I'm going to go out on a limb this once. To begin with, I'm sure you won't have any trouble finding another apartment. You can always stay with us temporarily until you do find something. You can have your old bedroom. As for a job, you're no slouch. I'm sure you'll be able to find an administrative assistant position somewhere. Why not ask Wild and Wonderful for a temporary position? After all, you're not the typical secretary/office assistant—you're very methodical and an excellent researcher. I'm sure Helen will be glad to have you back. Or at least ask her for a great recommendation."

Marcia started to interrupt, but Sammie held up her

hand to stop her.

"Hear me out. That wasn't the advice—only common sense stuff. This is the advice part." Her sister shook her head and pointed her finger for emphasis. "If I were you, I'd go to Rio without the dirty sleaze-ball." Sammie's hands doubled into fists, swiping at an imaginary Brad. "Take full advantage of the two-timing creep—take him for all he's worth. Or, at least what he's already paid out for the trip. He owes you, Sis. Big time. He broke your heart. You take you and your suitcases and those plane tickets and go to Rio without Brad. On his dime. Have a great time. Who knows, maybe you'll find a tall, dark, handsome Brazilian while you're there. Have fun, Marcia. Forget about Brad. Then come back home and deal with the rest of it."

"You're right, of course." She sighed, then wiped tears from her face with the back of her hands. "But I'm not sure I should go off by myself when I have so much to deal with at home."

Sammie handed her a tissue. She blew her nose, and then continued. "I guess finding another apartment won't be a problem, although finding another job might be more difficult. But I really can't go to Rio de Janeiro alone. It's *Carnaval* time, crowded, and I won't be comfortable going on my own—a single woman. Although"—she sniffed back another sob—"using the tickets so Brad can't use them to take his bimbo with him does sound like the perfect revenge."

She reached for the box of tissues on the counter next to the toaster. She really wasn't the type of person to exact revenge.

"Look, Sis, it's time you did something for you."

Her sister's voice softened. "And, you'd be sending the jerk a sound message—don't mess with me. Think about it. In the meantime, let me cut this banana bread so we can enjoy it with our coffee."

The phone rang as Sammie sliced into the warm, picture-perfect loaf she removed from the pan to cool.

"I'll get it for you." Marcia placed her cup back in the saucer and went to the phone on the wall behind the door. She checked the caller ID. "It's Beatrice. Wonder what she wants. I hope Heather is okay."

"Hi, Bea, how's my favorite sister-in-law?" Marcia drew in a deep breath to control her voice so as not to upset her brother's wife with her own problems. Beatrice and Russell had been having a hard time of it lately, their daughter Heather having had major medical problems over the last three years. They'd hardly been able to keep up financially, their house about to be swallowed up by foreclosure, as well.

"Oh, Marcia, I don't know what to do," Bea sobbed over the phone. "I don't want to worry you, what with your upcoming wedding and all, but I think Russell is in a lot of trouble. He's in Rio de Janeiro working for Jared. I got the strangest call from him. He sounded upset and very weird. You know your brother—nothing upsets him."

"Weird? How weird? What's wrong?"

Sammie ran to the living room and picked up the other phone.

"Beatrice? What is going on? What's wrong, sweetie?"

"It's Russell. He called from Rio an hour ago and sounded so upset. Something isn't right. I know it. He told me he had to stay as long as it took to clear his name. He was concerned he wouldn't be home in time for the wedding. Oh, Marcia, I know he feels awful about it, especially after the last fiasco you went through. His voice was very whispery, as if someone followed him or he didn't want to be overheard. He needs help. I know it. And I can't leave to go find out what's going on. Heather needs me here. And Russell needs someone there. What am I going to do?"

Leave it to Bea to worry about her wedding at a time like this. "First of all, Bea, don't worry about the wedding. I've called it off. I discovered Brad wasn't the one for me after all. I know, I know, it's a bit late, but at least I didn't make it to the church this time. So put that right out of your mind. Now, did you call his boss? I'm sure Mr. Reed will help if Russell is in trouble."

Marcia tried to reassure her sister-in-law. She had met Jared Reed two years ago. He might be a lot of things, but she'd always considered he was a fair employer who treated his employees and ranch hands with respect. She pictured Jared Reed in his cowboy get-up at his Double R Ranch in Oregon. One couldn't help but notice he was one sexy man. Tall, dark wavy hair, a grin that made you wonder what he was up to, and a muscular body were at odds with what one considered stereotypical of an owner of a technology company. But then she'd seen him dressed in his ranch clothes. And those brilliant cobalt-colored irises had looked deep into hers, and she had been lost. The image died as she recalled that he hadn't been that into her.

"Oh, Samantha, Russell made it very clear I wasn't to call Mr. Reed." Bea brought her back into the moment. "Do you think it has something to do with clearing his name? Something about selling out—and the Japanese? What do you think this all means? Oh, I'm so confused. I don't know what to do."

The fear in her sister-in-law's voice made the fine wispy hairs on her arm stand on end.

"There is only one way to find out. As I have a bit of time on my hands, I'll contact Mr. Reed and see if I can find out what the heck is going on."

Marcia didn't want to have anything to do with the man—face to face—after their first and last encounter. However, a phone conversation would be doable.

"Actually, Bea," Sammie interjected. "Marcia is going to go to Rio without Brad, so she can meet up with Russell and find out what's he's gotten himself involved in."

"What? Sammie!" Marcia exclaimed. "I don't think…"

"Oh, Marcia, thank you. That would be so great. You're the best sister-in-law anyone could ever have," Bea gushed over the line. "You too, Samantha. I'd feel so much better if you were there with him, Marcia. Make sure he's okay, give him your support. I feel like it's all my fault he went to Rio in the first place. He didn't want to go, but I told him we'd be able to manage on our own without him for a few days. Then I changed my mind, but it was too late."

"Don't blame yourself, Bea," Sammie sympathized over the phone. "No one is blaming anyone. Marcia will check it out. Everything is going to be fine."

Caught between a sister and a sister-in-law, Marcia didn't know which way to turn. Sure, Sammie's advice sounded great in theory. Going to Rio without Brad, albeit on his dime, was one thing. But going down to check up on her brother—it had all the makings of a spy movie, and she was no sleuth.

Could she hop a plane on her own and fly down to Rio? She wasn't a coward, but she wasn't stupid either. *Carnaval* was in full swing. However, with Russell meeting her at the airport, it might not be so daunting. Darn it, her brother had been through a lot lately—he didn't need this on top of everything else. Whatever "it" was.

"Tell me how to get in touch with him, and I'll arrange to have him meet me when I arrive." Marcia closed her eyes, held her breath, and then let it out. She'd go. It was the least she could do for her family— a family that had supported her over the years.

"Oh, thank you so much. You don't know what this means to me. To all of us. I only wish you were here so I could give both of you a big hug. I mean it, we've been so blessed."

It was just like Bea to overlook all the heartache they'd endured recently and feel thankful for what they still had. If only she could feel the same way in regards to her recent failed relationship with Brad-the-Rat!

****

Jared Reed sat behind his desk and shook his head. How the hell had this happened? And Russell? As his top marketing rep, he'd never questioned the man's integrity and service to the company.

The late afternoon sun filtered through his home office picture window. He tapped his pencil rapidly on his grandfather's old, well-worn oak desk. In a fit of anger, he threw the pencil to the side—it skidded and rolled to a stop against his oversized empty coffee mug.

"I'll be damned," he muttered, slapping his hand against his forehead.

"I was right wasn't I?" His longtime friend and technical assistant, Hank Johnson, pointed at the sheaf of papers strewn in front of them. He tapped them as if to lay claim to their importance.

"My God, Hank, I'm blown away by this. What…how…man. I don't even know what to say. What to think."

"I know. I felt the same way. At first, I thought I was delusional. Guess because he's so well liked, I turned a blind eye to the possibility. But then, I did some checking and hired a P.I. Here you have it in front of you as proof—in black and white, as they say."

"But can you prove he's the one sabotaging the company? Causing our sales to drop? How is he pulling this off?"

"Ah, the sixty-four-thousand-dollar question, isn't it? The figures the private dick gave me—what you see in front of you—means Russell is raking in the money—a lot of money—from somewhere. And with such a large amount, it can't be legal."

"Again, how the hell am I going to prove how he got a hold of it?"

"Look at these." Hank pointed to another sheet of calculated figures. "According to this bank statement, they've been in debt for the last five years, and last April the house was about to be foreclosed. Then, all of a sudden, it was totally paid up. We're talking about a loan of approximately $200,000. And their checking and savings account filled up three months later with $5,000 and $50,000 respectively. An enormous chunk of change, all considered."

"Look, Hank, I agree these documents look fishy as all get out. But I need proof he's stealing our prototypes and selling them behind our backs before I can do anything about it. I need to catch him in the act."

"I agree. You have a tough job ahead of you. Any ideas? You want me to contact this P.I. again and put him on the payroll?"

"Hold off. I'm not sure what I'm going to do, but I'm not going to sit on my hands and watch my company go down the tubes. We've all worked too hard over the years to make Reed Technologies, as well as the Double R Ranch, what it is today. We're not sunk yet."

He could have sworn Russell was an honest and above-board member of his team. He was a kind, considerate church-going family man and had never given the company any cause to be concerned about his dealings with foreign corporations.

Jared sighed and tapped his fingers on the desk. He bit at his bottom lip. "Good God! The timing couldn't be worse, what with our latest prototype ready to go into production next month."

"It's the perfect time for Russell to set things in motion with the Japanese and make another sale sure to undermine ours. I'm sorry to say this, Jared, but it looks as if sending Russell to Rio de Janeiro this past week has more than likely played right into his greedy hands."

"Damn." Jared shoved against the desk and shot back in his chair—it rolled backwards and hit the wall. "Looks to me as if he got in over his head and took the wrong way out."

"I see your point, but it doesn't excuse what he's doing."

"You're right, of course. Thanks for pointing all

this out and having your P.I. gather the documents together. Not sure what I plan to do with them, but they are evidence that will substantiate anything else I might be able to uncover."

Jared stood and walked to the window while his friend remained in the chair next to the desk with his hands dangling over the edge of his knees. He looked out over the Oregon mountains in the distance. He never tired of the vista surrounding his grandfather's Double R Ranch—his ranch—where he maintained his business headquarters for Reed Technologies. There was none of the hubbub of people, traffic, and nighttime noise of the city. Nothing but peace and quiet stretching for miles either side of his ranch. He swiveled around to face his long-time friend and assistant. "I think I'll schedule a trip to Rio. I feel the need to visit my brother to check on how his own computer company is doing in South America."

"Good idea. Russell is probably selling you into the ground as we speak." Hank rose from his chair and headed toward the door. "Let me know if there is anything else you need me to do."

"Sure thing. I'll see you at the gym around three-thirty this afternoon. We need to keep in shape for our rock-climbing expedition coming up in June. In the meantime, you can keep on top of things in the office while I'm away."

"Tell your brother 'hi' for me, and not to get too carried away during *Carnaval* this year."

"He learned his lesson last year. He ended up married to a hot samba dancer—she keeps him in line."

"I bet she does." Hank laughed, leaving the office and shutting the door behind him.

Jared strode back to the window. Thanks to his head technician, this was the best lead they'd had in a long time in trying to figure out how their Japanese competitor was able to develop the exact duplicate of their electronic interactive games months prior to their own releases hitting the stands. And, with a much cheaper price tag. Of course, the quality was nowhere near as good as Reed Technologies. While stock in the Japanese company soared, Jared's stock dipped. Drastically.

With their latest super DVD avatar game due to be released any day, this was the worst possible time for him to be away. Jared sighed, detached his cell phone from his clip, and punched in his brother's speed dial number. It didn't help that tourists would be flocking into Rio for *Carnaval*—the mobs would be horrendous and flights would be hard to come by. It was a good thing he had a private jet at his disposal.

Chapter Two

Russell wrung his hands to calm his shaking fingers. He took a moment before he opened the hotel room safe, tucked away at the bottom of the closet. The thumb drive with the avatar game on it that he'd formatted was fake. He'd played around with Jared's latest high-tech interactive game enough so the Japanese would think it was the latest up-and-coming release. Only trouble was, at the very end, he'd arranged for the entire game to disappear when the words "GAME OVER" appeared on the screen. He hoped Mr. Osaka would be forthcoming with more information about this Mr. Rose the two Brazilians had mentioned before he figured out the game was bogus. He didn't care about money changing hands, but he had to take it in order to make the deal. Make him look legit.

He prayed his plans didn't blow up in his face.

What was he going to do with three-quarters of a million dollars, anyway? Sure, there were things he'd like to do with the money, but he couldn't keep it. It was dirty money. Maybe a year ago he might have contemplated using it to get him and his family out from under all the medical bills they had accumulated for Heather. They had gotten behind in their mortgage payments on the house. Things had been pretty tough for a while. He hated to see what it was doing to Bea.

She was left to deal with their daughter and her health issues while he was travelling around the globe on behalf of Reed Technologies. But like a miracle from above, things had changed so fast it made their heads spin. Their financial woes were over, thanks to his local church holding a benefit on their behalf. On top of the already generous benefit, a large donation had come in from an anonymous donor, which had amounted to more than enough to get them out of debt and back on track.

Give him the flash drive and walk away. Find out what you can. Don't even worry about the money.

He slipped the tiny flash drive in his shorts pocket, and placed a note inside the safe in case things didn't go as planned. He didn't trust them. Anything could go wrong. He shut the heavy safe door and gave the dial a secure twist to make sure it was locked. He would call Bea after his meeting with Mr. Osaka, then wrap up his regular meeting with the Argentinean and Chilean businessmen and head home.

He walked to the window, hands in his pockets, and stared at the idyllic scenery, not seeing any of it. Wishing Bea and Heather were there to enjoy Rio with him, he wondered just what had been going on behind his back while he'd been dealing with his own family crises?

"I'm not sure how it happened, sweetheart," he'd told Bea over the phone when he'd first arrived in Rio. "Someone has put the word out that I'm cashing in by selling Jared's prototypes to the Japanese. I can't sit back any longer and let this happen."

Bea had been frantic. Wanted him to cancel his trip—to come home. He assumed he had convinced her he was doing the right thing. But she hadn't been so sure. She'd cried. He wished he hadn't called her, hadn't upset her. She'd been through too much already with Heather's blood disorder. Heck, they'd never heard of I.T.P.—an inadequate production of blood platelets. Neither of their families had ever suffered from the disease. At first, the doctors suggested it was a case of child abuse, her black and blue marks on her arms and legs an indication. It had broken their hearts to be accused of such a thing. Thankfully, their reverend had been aware of the signs, had stepped in, and convinced them to have the doctors do blood work. The results had them rushing Heather to the hospital for a blood transfusion when her blood platelets had dropped to dangerous levels. The count was so low they'd been about to lose their precious daughter.

Russell sighed, grabbed his sunglasses, and headed out the door. He punched the elevator's down button, and then slipped inside when the doors swished open. He poked the lever for the lobby, took deep breaths to calm his shaking nerves, wiped the sweat from his forehead, and prayed all would go as planned.

The brilliance of the bright late afternoon sunshine was blinding. He withdrew his sunglasses from his tropical, paisley print shirt pocket and slipped them in place. He hoped he fit in with the rest of the tourists scattered along the beach. He crossed the street and headed south along the sidewalk until he came to a large ornate sand art sculpture depicting a shark with sharp teeth, a sand castle in the center, and a half naked mermaid stretched out to one side. "Welcome to Rio" was etched on the border of the sand castle. The artist sat in a beach chair equipped with an umbrella, a jug on a stand close by for donations. He nodded, dropped a few coins in the glass bottle, and walked on by, his mind focused on his mission.

After another five hundred yards, Russell stepped onto the white sandy beach and headed toward the ocean. To the left was a small deserted cluster of palm trees where he had been instructed to meet Mr. Osaka. He searched the area—no one. He checked his watch. The minute hand clicked on the hour. Not knowing what to do, he continued toward the small oasis, his sandals kicking up granules of white hot sand as he strode to the shaded spot. A slight breeze fanned his hair, and the salty ocean spray clung to his bare legs. Instead of enjoying the tropical ambiance, he shivered. Hesitant, he drew closer, scanning the area. Where was Mr. Osaka?

Russell circled the palms. Was he in the wrong place? Had Mr. Osaka changed his mind? Thinking perhaps someone decided to play games with him and was hiding in among the trees, he inched his way in between the tight grouping of palms. A note, not hard to miss, was tacked to the trunk of one of the center trees. Mr. Rose's name was clearly scrawled in thick black letters across the envelope.

Who was this Rose person?

Baffled, he plucked the metal thumbtack from the bark, opened the envelope, and extracted a thick piece of folded paper.

Meet me at Confeiteria Colombo
Rua Gonçalves Dias, 32 Centro
19:00 hrs.

Russell checked his watch—with traffic congestion during *Carnaval*, it was obvious he didn't have enough time to hail a taxi and make his way into Rio's Old Town and the historic coffee house. He stared out over the glistening water. Things weren't working out the way he thought they would. No matter what happened from here on out, he had to warn Jared what was happening behind his back.

Russell walked back to the hotel, wrote a note to Jared, filling him in on what he'd learned so far, warning him who to look out for, and mentioning Mr. Osaka's name as a person of interest in the Japanese scheme. For good measure, he inserted the thumb-drive with the fake game into the thick envelope before mailing it at the post office.

He hailed a taxi.

"Confeiteria Colombo, please."

****

Maybe flying to Rio by herself without making contact with Russell first wasn't such a good idea after all. Not being able to contact Jared Reed wasn't a good sign either.

Marcia looked around the airport only to find several love-sick couples milling around her as if they were the only ones in the crowded terminal. Waiting to identify her luggage as it arrived on the revolving conveyor belt in the baggage claim area, she tried to ignore several handsome men rubbing their hands soothingly along their sexy partner's backs—a nuzzle along their necks here, a full-blown kiss there. Arms cradled slender waists of young ladies and women dressed in strappy heels and cool, slinky dresses. There was so much love in the air she was tempted to hop back on the plane and go home. But she had promised Bea she'd look for Russell, meet with him, and find out what had him acting so strange and secretive. What kind of trouble had he gotten himself into in Rio. Make sure he was okay.

Marcia sighed. She shouldn't have listened to Sammie. She shouldn't have let Bea play the sympathy card. They had both caught her at a depressing moment. She'd been too blinded by despair at the time to seriously consider her sister's sage advice. However, the more she had time to mull it over, the more she had realized Sammie did have a point—Brad owed her. And really, there was no way—if push came to shove—she would refuse to help her brother.

She spotted her single check-in suitcase, ran for it, and lifted it from the conveyor belt before it made another circle and a chance for someone else to claim it by mistake. Edging in between others trying to do the same thing, loaded down with her carryon, made it more difficult. She managed to snatch it in time, wheel it to the side, attach the carryon to the top of her bag, and proceed to the customs area. Once through the long line, she made her way out the front door into the blinding sunshine and hot air. The tantalizing scent of the ocean hung in the early evening breeze. Catching her breath and her bearings, she hailed a taxi to take her to the hotel. After a scenic drive along the bay with Sugar Loaf Mountain dramatically rising up on the other side, the driver maneuvered the vehicle to a stop in front of the Iberostar Copacabana Hotel along the Avenida Atlantica. She had to hand it to Brad, the hotel had been his choice, and it turned out to be spectacular, and one of many located prominently across the street from the famed Copacabana beachfront. In a flurry of haste, bellhops assisted her. Registration taken care of, she was whisked up to the honeymoon suite on the top floor. Her luggage deposited inside the room, the young, tanned, handsome porter nodded, a broad grin on his face, shut the door on his way out.

Left alone, Marcia stood in stunned appreciation at the opulence of the accommodation. She kicked off her shoes and sighed as her feet sank into the deep pile of the white, wall-to-wall carpet. Ignoring her luggage, she wound her way over to the window past the plush mauve loveseat, the easy chairs, and the low glass-topped table overflowing with fresh fruit displayed in an ornate wicker basket. A large crystal vase with blood-red sweetheart roses filled the stand next to the window. The fragrance overwhelmed her senses. Tears pooled at the back of her eyes and threatened to spill over her cheeks. Her bottom lip trembled. She looked out at the sprawling Copacabana Beach and the incredible panoramic view. The picture-perfect small copse of coconut trees, cerulean sea, and sun-bleached sand couldn't be denied. Her deep sigh morphed into a smile. How could she not respond to such sensual surroundings? The water lapped against the shore, couples lazed on the sand under an azure sky—it all called to her inner romantic. Before she could change her mind, she threw her linen dress jacket over the pale green chair, and snapped her suitcase open. She rifled through the contents, which she'd neatly organized a couple of weeks ago in anticipation of her honeymoon, and dug out a lightweight pale melon colored tank top, beige Capri pants, and a pair of strappy flats. She glanced at the sexy nightclothes and bikini she'd anticipated wearing for Brad, shut the suitcase and changed her clothes.

His loss.

She tucked a small wallet with all the necessary items in her front pocket—room key-card, ID/Passport, some change, her sunglasses. It took seconds to knot her hair back in a French twist, and secure it with a single hair comb before heading out the door.

Bradley or no Bradley, she'd be darned if she was going to waste another minute locked in a hotel room in Rio de Janeiro, pining away for a man who clearly didn't love her. Had cheated on her days before their wedding.

The warmth of the late afternoon sun and the soft breeze off the rolling waves soothed her. She stood in queue at the crosswalk waiting for the light to change green. Crossing the separate streets going in opposite directions was tricky, but Marcia followed the crowd when the signal changed and the timed crossing ticker ticked down. She stepped up onto the gray and white tiled sidewalk, designed to depict waves. It reminded her of zebra stripes. The tropical breeze washed over her. She couldn't help but linger as she passed the numerous vendors selling various local items. From handcrafted jewelry to t-shirts to fruit drinks, it all added to the touristy festive atmosphere of Rio, as did the music from the outdoor restaurants and bars along the strip. But she wasn't in the mood to do any shopping. She slipped her shoes off and headed straight for the waves lapping the shoreline. The early evening sun was still brilliant overhead. The sand burned hot under her feet—the water soothing when her toes splashed along the crashing waves. The scent of the various suntan lotions on tanned bodies drifted across the beach. A few volleyball games were in progress, and couples and even children walked or frolicked in the water.

Taking a deep breath, Marcia lifted her face to the azure sky, caught up in the tropical breeze, the salty smell of the ocean, and the brilliance of the sun as it began its afternoon descent. Her spirits plummeted almost as quickly as they had soared—she should be walking hand in hand, sharing all this with Brad. They should be strolling happily ever after, not a care in the world, like those walking the shoreline. But thanks to his cheating soul, it had all came crashing down around her. Angry with herself for being duped, being the proverbial last to know, she'd had no recourse but to dump the jerk. Did he deserve a second chance?

Not in her lifetime.

As she continued to wander down the beach, her mind wandered back to the incident that had put an end to her happily ever after. She'd just been to the caterer, excited about tasting samples of hors d'oeuvres for their wedding reception, and hadn't been able to wait to share them with Brad. The chef had agreed to package up some of the morsels so she could surprise Brad with a picnic lunch in his office. The pastry-chef had provided her with a small basket complete with a handle for ease of transport. She'd felt like Dorothy in the Wizard of Oz on her way home from the wicked witch. Little did she know she was heading straight toward disaster and a wicked witch in the form of her aerobics instructor. After stopping at the local liquor store to pick up a bottle of white zinfandel, she walked another block to Brad's office, ready for an impromptu romantic lunch.

She took the elevator to the top floor where Brad

had his offices. Expecting to see Mary Sue, his receptionist, she was surprised to find the reception area empty. Usually Mary Sue ate lunch at her desk to take calls. Perhaps Brad had given her time off for a special occasion.

Marcia walked past Mary Sue's desk, down the hallway to Brad's office. Out of courtesy, she gave his closed door a gentle knock, shifted the basket to her left hand, and with her free hand, twisted the knob, then stepped inside. He wasn't at his desk. Her shoulders slumped. She hugged the basket tight against her stomach and sighed. She glanced around the dim opulent room, and froze. Her gasp echoed in the stillness of the shaded office. Brad's long, lean, naked body lay sprawled on top of an equally naked woman on the black leather sofa along the far wall. The woman lounged under Brad in a very sexual position. They were engrossed in a very passionate kiss. The woman slowly finished the embrace with a lingering pull on Brad's lower lip. She turned her head, her eyes darting across the room, brimming with an after-glow that should have been Marcia's. The woman wore a smug, satisfied, wide smile on a blemish-free, peaches and cream, young face.

The face of her aerobics instructor. Brad's face, on the other hand, was hidden in the valley of the woman's plentiful breasts. His shoulders slumped forward as if to cover his lover from the eyes of the intruder.

"I told you not to interrupt us, Mary Sue," he growled, his voice muffled.

He hadn't even had the decency to sound embarrassed—simply annoyed.

"It's not Mary Sue, lover," the blonde bimbo

laughed, sliding her bare leg over the back of Brad's equally bare leg. "It's your fiancé."

Marcia wanted to wipe the sexual predator grin off the girl's face.

The two-timing cheat groaned, but didn't budge a single muscle.

Marcia's insides clenched wondering if his groan was due to sexual arousal or the fact he'd been interrupted. Her hand fisted in front of her clenched lips, she backed out the door.

"Marcia, wait," he finally called out, his voice more exasperated than pleading. "It's not what you think."

"Are you serious?" She swirled around and gave him a glare she hoped he'd understand. "It's exactly what I think."

She took great satisfaction in slamming the door on her way out. Effectively shutting out the site of the two of them entwined in each other's arms.

But not out of her mind.

Did he think she was blind? Ignorant? Stupid?

"We need to talk," he yelled through the closed door. "Give me a minute. Wait for me in reception."

"You've got to be joking," she'd hissed through clenched teeth. Did he really think her gullible enough to hang around while he searched for his pants and put them on so they could talk?

By the time she approached the elevator, he was beside her, tucking in his shirttails. She punched the elevator call button and stood with her back to him.

"Nothing you can say is ever going to change my mind. The wedding is off."

He grabbed her arm, twirled her around to face

him, but before he could voice a single protest, she'd put her hand up in his face to stop him.

"Apparently you can't hear while under the influence of cheating on me. So, let me repeat myself. *We. Are. Through.* We have nothing to discuss."

"Yes, we do—I can explain…"

"No. You can't."

Her mind did double time on what she'd like to do to Brad—every one of which was illegal and not worth landing in jail.

The elevator door swished open. She shot in like a bullet, then jabbed the button for the lobby, thankful the door only stayed open a brief second—the longest second she'd ever had to endure. She glared at Brad as he stood in the hallway looking at her with lost, puppy-dog eyes as if he really cared she was about to walk out on him. Like it would work, and she'd go running back into his arms. What did he expect her to do? Get down on bended knees and plead with him to love her and not her sexy bimbo of an aerobics instructor he'd just had sex with? Wait in the reception area while he and his lover got dressed, kissed, and said their goodbyes?

Not in this lifetime.

The man was delusional to think she was ever going to be able to wipe the nauseating sight out of her mind—or ever sit on a black leather sofa again. She was only glad she had discovered the true Brad before they'd tied the knot.

The two-timing rat!

No longer able to stand walking the beach alone, Marcia went back to her hotel room. Dialing the hotel number Bea had given her, she called Russell, again. No answer. Worried Bea might be right, and Russell really was in trouble, she quickly showered and changed into a lightweight pair of tan slacks, and a cotton short-sleeved teal blouse. She slipped into a pair of comfortable flats, and grabbed a light wrap. Throwing the straps of her purse over her shoulder, she slid her sunglasses over her forehead into her hair for easy access when she hit the bright evening sun. She made her way down to the lobby to go in search of her brother.

According to Bea's directions, Russell's hotel was only a couple blocks away from her own hotel. However, once on the boardwalk, she discovered, not only was the hotel farther than expected, but it was three blocks into the fabric of the "real" Rio de Janeiro behind the posh landscape of the many five-star hotels lining the miles of white sandy beaches.

Marcia rounded a corner and walked down the side street. She passed a juice bar with patrons lined up to place their orders, and those walking away with tall juicy drinks—several of whom were dressed provocatively in bright sequined outfits and painted faces. It was a reminder *Carnaval* was in full swing. Crossing another narrow intersection with giant buildings either side of the street and overcrowded sidewalks, it didn't take her long to feel closed in. The uncomfortable feeling of being followed persisted as she searched for Russell's hotel.

Marcia stopped before she crossed another intersection and did a thorough search of the pedestrians. The only person looking out of place was a tall, white male wearing a white short-sleeved shirt, a baseball cap, and a pair of reflective sun glasses. The man, although athletically built, didn't seem a threat.

Taking a deep breath, she crossed the street and concentrated on looking for Russell's building. Spotting it up ahead, she was about to cross the street when someone grabbed her arm and shoved her up against the side of the building. He snatched her shoulder bag with gloved fingers. She tugged back, but his heavy hooded body crushed her against the stucco building, and she was unable to free her arm in order to fight off the attacker. Something sharp jabbed her ribs. Marcia's knees buckled.

Chapter Three

Jared couldn't believe his good luck. Spotting Marcia Kline in Rio de Janeiro had his heart racing. He remembered the last time they'd met. She was even more beautiful than two years ago when they'd parted, albeit not on friendly terms. Being Russell's sister, he'd put his feelings aside, not wanting to ruin a good employee-employer relationship with one of his best marketing reps. He hadn't been ready for a permanent relationship—his company had been on the brink of breaking even, his latest avatar game about to go viral. He hadn't had time for a personal relationship, and it had been obvious Marcia was interested in forever. He didn't figure he was the one who could give her what she wanted. Now...well, now things had changed. But not for the better. Hell, her brother was in the process of selling the company's secrets.

He followed Marcia down the side street wondering where she was headed. What was she doing in Rio? Was she here with Russell? Were they in cahoots together? Thinking Marcia might lead him to her brother, he followed her, his mind drifting to their last encounter. It'd been at one of his company's family barbecues he'd thrown at his ranch. She'd been visiting her brother and his family, and had attended the event. He smiled, remembering the moment he had spotted her. She'd been confident, friendly, and outgoing. Not to mention a knock-out with her understated full figure, long blonde hair swept back in a sexy ponytail. Her mesmerizing, dazzling blue eyes the shade of seduction. He'd been surprised someone hadn't snapped her up the way she'd been attentive to her brother's family. She'd even spent time playing games with the children— laughing, having a ball. He hadn't been able to take his eyes off her. She eyed him as well, and had his heart doing flip-flops. He had asked her out. She'd accepted. They dated twice, and it had not ended the way she had hoped—she'd been looking for permanence. He hadn't.

Still wasn't.

Why was she wandering these back streets on her own? He recalled Russell mentioning she was engaged to be married? Was she here with her husband? Where the hell was he? What kind of jerk was he, letting her walk the back streets of Rio by herself?

Baffled, he inched closer, and then caught a short, rough-looking, dark-skinned Brazilian dogging her steps. The man suddenly grabbed Marcia's arm and shoved her into the side of the building. Jared raced across the street, yanked the man away and caught her just as she was about to crash to the pavement. He stepped in, jostled her to the side, away from the crowded street.

"Are you crazy, woman? Don't you know how dangerous it is wandering these streets on your own?"

"What? Who…? Jared?" She gasped, finally recognizing him. She yanked her arm free and gave him a glare promising evil intent. "What are you doing following me?"

She shrank back as if he'd been the attacker. His insides blanched at the absurd idea.

"I'm not the one following you. In case you weren't aware, the man who disappeared through the crowd on the other side of the street was hot on your heels and the one who attacked you. What the hell are you doing alone in this part of town, anyway?"

"None of your business."

He wasn't sure if it was anger or fright coming from her baby blues. Perhaps both.

He held her gaze for a long moment. She stood her ground. Was there a touch of sadness or fear she hid beneath her lowered long, sexy eyelashes? It didn't matter. He had to get her out of the back streets. She might as well have a target pasted on the middle of her back—she was like a sitting duck in the middle of a wide-opened pond. For the love of Pete, the place crawled with *Carnaval* crazies.

"Listen, I didn't mean to startle you. But, really, this is a very unsavory side of Rio you don't want to get caught up in alone. I'll walk you out."

"Don't bother. I'm not leaving."

Her quick recovery, resolve, and confidence were a surprise. He raised his eyebrows.

"Let me reiterate—are you crazy, woman?"

The woman gave exasperating a new meaning. Was she really that naïve not to be aware of the danger surrounding her?

"You were just accosted, for God's sake." He couldn't help reinforcing the reality of what had happened.

"Listen, Mr. Reed…."

"Jared."

"*Jared.* If you'll excuse me, I'll be on my way."

"Then let me escort you to your destination.

Which, I hope, for your sake isn't much further."

"Too kind of you to worry, *Jared*...but, like I explained, I can manage on my own."

"Nevertheless, I insist."

Her breasts rose seductively as she took in a deep breath of resignation. His gut clenched, he held his own breath. Once again, she was a distraction he didn't need. He let his breath out between tight lips and looked away for a moment.

"Where are you headed?"

He could tell she didn't want to answer his question. Too bad. He had all night.

"Marcia...?" he coaxed.

She hesitated a moment longer. His patience was about shot—one thing he usually had plenty of. Usually. But this trip to Rio wasn't for fun and games. He was after her brother to put a stop to him selling the company's top sales digital tech games to the Japanese.

And then it hit him. She was on her way to see Russell, too. Was she involved in his criminal activities? Was that why she was in Rio walking down the back streets? To meet up with her brother in secret and plan their next hand-off?

Shit! He'd never consider her to have criminal tendencies. But then, he hadn't expected Russell to be that kind of man, either.

"Looking for your brother?"

Her head shot up. *Bingo!*

"None of your business," she repeated, rushed past him, and started walking down the street.

"Not so fast, lady," he smiled, stepped alongside her, and matched her angry strides. "As I'm heading in the same direction myself, I'm more than happy to make sure you get there—safe and sound."

"Not necessary."

She kept her eyes forward, slipped around several women loaded down with packages. She held her back straight, her head high, and picked up her pace. The woman had attitude written all over her. He smiled, liking the entire package, despite the bad timing. It didn't take much to maintain his pace. However, his height and long strides matched hers with ease.

"I'm not sure why Russell wanted to stay in one of the smaller hotels buried way back in this god-awful district. I make sure my employees have a sufficient expense account when they travel. I don't skimp when it comes to promoting the company."

"I'm sure you don't."

He wasn't sure what she meant with her terse remark, but he let that one go.

"So, what are you doing in Rio de Janeiro all on your own?" He kept watch of the crowded street as he continued to walk by her side.

"None of—"

"I know. *None of my business.* That's getting old already."

"Then don't ask me any more questions that are—"

"*None of my business.* I get it. Ah, here's his hotel. Pretty unsavory looking if you ask me."

She had to agree. She had been in a secure bubble of her own making walking around Rio alone. After she'd been accosted, not to mention Jared scaring the crap out of her when he'd grabbed her arm and shoved her aside, she hated to admit she was relieved to have him walking at her side.

Jared followed her up the dark, seedy interior

staircase, making her feel self-conscious knowing his eyes were level with her backside. She didn't want to feel anything for Jared Reed. If she actually counted him, she'd been rejected three times. Thankfully, she and Jared had never gotten as far as the altar. More to the point, they had never made it any further than heavy seductive caresses. Oh, my, what his hands had done to her body. What his kisses had made her feel—want to do.

Her shoe caught on the next to the last step. She tripped, her hands shooting forward to catch her fall. Warm, firm hands wrapped around her hips. She was upright before she hit the floor. Good thing she faced forward—the warmth seeping into her face was too hot not to be noticeable. She wouldn't be able to blame it on sunburn, seeing as she hadn't had a chance to lie on the beach and soak up the rays.

Jared dropped his hands, and she continued down the hall. She found room twenty-seven and knocked on the door. Jared leaned on the wall next to the doorframe, his eyes concentrating on the well-worn, dirty carpet as if it held the answers to the universe hidden in what was left of the stained low pile.

The hallway was damp, smelled of tobacco, booze, and cleaning fluid, which didn't quite mask the musky odors. What had Russell been thinking staying in a place like this?

She knocked again.

Still, no answer.

Jared, leaning against the wall, swung his right arm up and pounded on the door so hard the sound echoed off the dingy walls. With raised eyebrows, she shook her head and gave him an "are you kidding me" look.

She expected to see a hole in the brittle wooden door.

He ignored her.

"Russell. It's Jared. Open up," he shouted, making her jump.

"I don't think he's in," she sighed.

"Let's find out."

She started back down the hall.

"Where do you think you're going?" he called after her.

She stopped, swung around, hands on hips, and stared into his enquiring eyes. "To get someone to open the door for us—a key." She pointed at the closed door. "You have a better idea?"

"Actually…yes. Stand back."

He stepped in front of the door, kicked it open with a decisive thunk. The door swung wide, hitting the wall on the other side with a bang.

"What the hell are you doing?" she hissed.

He stepped aside, a twisted smile on his satisfied face, and held the door open.

"You can't just bust down a door to find out if someone is inside. You want to get us arrested and thrown in jail?"

"You really think someone is going to call the police in a hovel of an establishment such as this?" He stepped inside without waiting for an answer, and froze. *"Holy shit!"* he yelled, putting his hands up to stop her from entering.

"What? What's wrong?"

Marcia bumped into his back and then peered around his big frame to see what had him stopping just inside the room. Her mouth dropped open, her eyes popped wide. Disbelief washed over her. She stood rigid, unable to utter a single word.

"Either Russell is a slob, or..." Jared shook his head.

"He's not," she whispered. "Oh, my, God! What happened? Are you sure we have the right room?"

It looked as if a cyclone had hit. Even the bed was tossed on its side, the bedding tangled along the wall of the miniscule room with the stuffing yanked out of it. Nothing had been left untouched.

"What the hell is your brother involved in?" He walked around the room, not touching anything.

"There's got to be a mistake," she whispered.

Then it hit her. Russell's room had been broken into and searched. Not neatly, mind you, but searched in a crazed, uncaring manner by the looks of the chaos confronting them.

"What's going on, Jared? Who did this? Why did Russell call Bea and tell her he might be in danger?"

"He's in danger?" he threw back, sounding skeptical. "That's not the way I understand it."

"Then you're wrong."

She didn't know what he'd been told, but without a doubt her brother was innocent.

She scanned the same area Jared had checked out. These were definitely Russell's belongings—his briefcase the family had put together and gotten him when he'd started working at Reed Technologies. Slashed. A black suit jacket—the drycleaner's tag still stapled to the garment bag, which hung like a drunkard on a binge.

A loud gasp from the doorway startled her. She and Jared turned at the same time. A dark-haired man quickly made a fast exit down the hall. Jared beat her to the door and sprinted after the man. Marcia followed, only to bump into Jared's back again when he stopped in the middle of the hall.

"Who? Where'd he go?"

The man had vanished.

"I'm not sure, but it's the same man who followed and attacked you in the street. And I have no idea where he went. It's as if he was a ghost."

She rubbed her arms. The thin wrap she'd put on before leaving her hotel room didn't quite quell the goose bumps running up and down her skin with Jared's ghost reference.

"If you're ready to leave, I'll escort you back to your hotel. I assume you're staying on the avenue."

"What do you think he was looking for?" She headed toward the staircase. "Do you think he found it?"

"If it was here to begin with, I suspect it isn't here any longer. As for our intruder, I think he was as surprised as we were to find the place searched. Not to mention finding us standing in the middle of Russell's hotel room."

He didn't elaborate on what the man was looking for. Piqued at his dodging her question, she poked his elbow to gain his attention. He ignored her and kept on walking down the hall. She yanked hard this time, stopping him in his tracks. Not an easy thing to do; the man was solid—tall, well-toned, handsome, and sexy as all get out. Just touching him revived memories of being held against his body and the kisses they'd shared. Kisses that had ended all too soon. He'd made it very clear he didn't want a long term relationship. She hadn't been looking for a one-night stand. She'd walked away.

And hadn't seen Jared since. Until today.

"What were they looking for, Jared? What would Russell have that would cause someone to tear his room apart like this? And where is Russell?"

Without his sunglasses shading his eyes—very sexy, bedroom eyes—Jared looked deep into hers, one eyebrow raised as if she knew the answers to her own questions.

"Jared?"

"We can't talk here. Someone might be listening."

He took her arm and escorted her down the corridor. As if to prove his point, two young obviously inebriated youths clunked up the stairs, laughing, staring at them, their Portuguese slurred. She let Jared put his arm around her as if they were a couple. They walked down the stairs together. At the bottom of the staircase a young couple stumbled in—barely clothed and obviously having been out celebrating *Carnaval*. They swayed past in their own world.

It was darker when they exited the building—the air warm, but cooler, the evening breeze playing with her hair. The street appeared more sinister, with everything in shadow. The crowded throng was more raucous. She appreciated Jared's arm around her shoulders. She clung to him like a lover as they walked through the back streets into the open avenue along the beachfront. Outdoor cafés stretched along the street were filled with the late dinner crowd. Tantalizing odors of spicy meats, potatoes, and other savory foods reminded Marcia she hadn't eaten since she'd picked at the meager food service on the plane. As much as she'd like to settle at one of the cafés, she wasn't about to become a sitting duck. Thankfully, she'd crammed a couple energy bars in her carry-on—they would help get her through the night once she got back to the hotel. Heck, she might just order room service so she wouldn't have to go out again. After all, it was on Brad's dime.

"As much as it might seem cozy sitting out in the open, talking over drinks, I don't want to stop in plain sight," Jared said, as if reading her mind. "Which way to your hotel? We can talk there without being interrupted."

At least they were on the same wavelength as far as safety was concerned. Spending time in her hotel room with him, however, was a different matter altogether. Despite her sister telling her to have a "good time" in Rio without Brad, she wasn't up for a one-night stand with Jared Reed. And, as much as she'd love to get even with Brad, she wasn't up for rebound sex with someone else out of spite. Not that it would have any effect on Brad whatsoever—after all, he had Ms. Bimbo the aerobics instructor for entertainment.

And he was welcome to her.

Jared slid his arm down her back. Before he could encircle her waist, she stepped aside. They continued the several blocks in silence. When they arrived at her room's entrance, he took the keycard from her shaking fingers and inserted it, then shoved the door open. He stepped aside so she could enter. She flicked the light switch on and froze for the second time that night. She swayed. Her knees buckled. Jared caught her before she hit the floor.

"Oh, shit. Not again," he groaned.

The room was in shambles.

Jared tugged her into his strong arms.

"Steady," he whispered, and proceeded to guide her through the door on the right into the bathroom. He put the seat down on the commode, sat her down, and then shut the door. "Are you okay?"

"Why?" Her voice wobbled. "Why me?" *What was Russell involved in?* "What are they looking for? I don't have anything."

"Well, at least this answers our question of whether or not they found what they were looking for in Russell's room. Are you sure you don't know what they're after? Think, Marcia," he insisted. "Someone must believe you have something they want. Otherwise, why search your room, too? What did you pack in your luggage?"

He took a white fluffy washcloth from the rack on the wall, ran it under the cold water, wrung it out, and handed it to her. With trembling hands, she rubbed the cool cloth over her hot face. As hot as her face had grown, the rest of her shivering body was ice-cold with fear.

"Nothing. Honest, Jared," she stuttered. "I didn't even bring my iPad on this trip. I figured if I needed to get in touch with anyone, I'd call."

"What about Russell? How did you know where to find him?"

He leaned against the washbasin counter, crossed his arms and waited. She looked up and met his eyes, their knees within inches of touching. The room shrunk around them as he towered over her.

"His wife called me, asked me to check in on him while I was in Rio."

"And what are you doing in Rio?"

"Does it matter? The important thing is—where is Russell? I wasn't able to contact him before I left New York. I called when I got in, but there was still no answer. As you can see, he wasn't in his room when I went to call on him tonight."

She didn't want Jared to find out about her sad excuse of a honeymoon for one, and that she was there on her own. She didn't need him, or anyone else feeling sorry for her because she'd caught her fiancé with another woman. She could feel sorry for herself all on her own.

"Well, you can't stay in this room," he surprised her, not waiting for an answer. "It isn't safe." He put his hands in his pants pockets and shook his head.

"You're right, I can't stay here. I don't want to." She sighed, and rose. "I'll see if I can get another room."

About to speak, he hesitated, then stood and took hold of her hands. He slid his long fingers around her wrists and tugged her up into his arms. He quickly dropped his arms to his side, stepped back, and then nodded as if he had come to a decision.

"I'll call the front desk, let them know what's going on. Have them call the police. Afterwards, you can pack your bags. My brother has a large house in the suburbs. I'm sure his wife Sophia will be happy for the company. You can stay with them until we get things figured out."

"But…"

"You want to stay here?"

"No."

"Then it's settled. I'll give Kurt a call. Let them know we're coming."

He gently helped her from the too small bathroom, stepped over the bedding littering the floor and picked up the phone sitting on its side, the receiver dangling over the edge. She didn't pay attention to his phone call. Instead, she circled the room checking to see if anything was missing.

She spied her unmentionables—the sexy nightgown she had anticipated wearing for Brad. She picked it up and let it slip through her fingers.

"Don't touch anything," Jared snapped, then returned to his call.

She dropped the flimsy garment as if it burned her hands. It floated to the floor. Embarrassment warmed her cheeks, and she lowered her head, not wanting Jared to see how flustered she was over being caught with such sexy items in her hand. She stepped to the side of the bed and looked around the room. She hadn't unpacked her toiletries, but like the other contents in her luggage, they were haphazardly strewn everywhere.

What did they think she was hiding? What were they looking for? What had Russell gotten himself into?

"Are you sure?" Jared exclaimed to whoever was on the other end of the phone.

She faced him and found puzzled eyes—and that sexy raised eyebrow staring back at her. "Kline. The last name is Kline. Marcia Kline."

"Holcomb," she stated, heat flooding her face for the second time in a matter of minutes. He raised the other eyebrow.

"Holcomb," he said into the mouthpiece, never taking his eyes off her. "Yes, room 1036. Bradley Holcomb?"

She nodded to confirm his question and settled in

the chair next to the window. She gazed out at the moonlight, not wanting to see the shock on his face.

He hung up the phone and sank into the chair opposite her. "If you're married, where's Mr. Holcomb?"

"If you must know, I have no idea."

"Is he with you here in Rio?"

"No. He's back in New York. We're not married."

Damn! Now he was aware of what a pathetic loser she really was—going on a honeymoon without the groom.

Chapter Four

The lights twinkled brightly behind them as Jared drove away from the hotel.

After a half-hearted grueling encounter with the police, the officer in charge had dismissed the situation seeing as nothing was stolen. Attributing the incident to *Carnaval*, Marcia was allowed to finish packing and leave. When she told them her brother's apartment had also been broken into and he was missing, they again blamed *Carnaval* and intimated, with a meaningful half-grin, he would show up eventually. Jared hadn't forced the issue, but had given the officers his contact information in case they found any leads or needed more information.

Marcia wasn't hopeful. She sighed as Jared maneuvered the car into the line of traffic.

"I thought we'd stop for something to eat before we go to my brother's. He lives at the other side of Rio in the Barra de Tijuca suburb. People there call it the Barra district. The future Rio—a bit more American with its *Gávea* golf course, condominiums, large shopping mall and entertainment complexes along the beach. São Conrado is close by. Perhaps we can go hang gliding while you're here."

"I've never hang glided before. I'm not sure I'm up to it."

"Plenty of time to think about it."

"Where are we headed?" She took in the throng of tourists mixed with locals wandering the streets and beach where volleyball games were finishing for the night. Further along a group of locals rolled up their beach mats after having performed their evening synchronized exercises. Lovers strolled hand in hand along the sidewalk, and several lingered under palm trees for an embrace. Traffic was slow and heavy. Syncopated Brazilian tunes from the open bars and restaurants echoed on the evening breeze.

"I know a great Brazilian café in the old part of town—Largo da Carioca. There's an historic café called the Confeiteria Colombo. It's very popular. It'll be crowded on the main floor this time of night, but we can talk without being overheard on the upper level. I called ahead for a reservation."

He'd been busy on the phone while she'd been gathering her belongings. Her nerves had her so worked up, her mouth was dry. And even though she hadn't eaten all day, she didn't think she could swallow her own saliva, let alone think about getting food down her throat at the moment. She quietly gazed out the side window. Her first day in Rio had certainly been a memorable one. Not in the way she had wanted, but memorable all the same. She crossed her fingers that they would find Russell, and that he was okay, so she could get on with her plans to enjoy her time in Rio.

"You okay over there?" Jared covered her hand in his. Heat waves zinged up her arm and shot right to her heart. She pulled her hand away.

"I know this has been upsetting."

If he only knew. Being alone and attacked in a foreign country where someone had broken into both her and her brother's rooms, leaving her homeless in Rio, in lieu of a better term, with the possibility of her brother's life being in danger, was much more than upsetting. It was downright terrifying.

"Marcia?"

"What do you think? I'm a single female being stalked for no apparent reason. My brother's hotel room has been ransacked. My hotel room was trashed as well. Every hotel room in all of Rio is booked due to *Carnaval*. I'm hotel-less. My finances are limited, and my ticket home won't be honored until ten days from now. Hell, no. I'm not okay."

She wasn't going to throw the lack of a job, a home, a marriage, and a real honeymoon to the mix of her problems. They had nothing to do with Jared.

Her hands shook. She knotted them in her lap and took a couple steadying breaths trying to stay calm. She had a strong desire to pound her fists on the dashboard. Her life was falling apart more and more every time she turned around. And on top of that, she had no idea how she was going to tell her sister-in-law that her husband—her brother—was missing, his room broken into and the possibility he might have been kidnapped. Or worse—killed.

"You're not homeless. Kurt and Sophia are happy to have you stay with them while you remain in Rio."

Staying with Jared's family was the last place she wanted to crash. Not only had she made a fool of herself two years ago, thinking there was something between Jared and herself, she was sure he was out to get Russell and blame him for whatever was going on down here in Rio. What would his family think of her?

"I appreciate their offer, but I'm sure if I look hard

enough I'll find another hotel room somewhere."

"It's *Carnaval*. Everything is full up to overflowing. I'm surprised you managed a room on the beach as it is."

"We made reservations a year ago—didn't want to take any chances."

"Don't worry. Like I said, my brother's place is big enough for an entire family. And his wife loves company."

"If you're sure it won't be an imposition?"

"Not a problem. I'm staying there as well. I planned to take a few days away from the office while I looked into things. I will be more than happy to escort you around Rio. Let me know what's on your agenda, and I'll see you get there."

Oh. My. God. Could her situation get any worse? She hadn't intended to take advantage of the entire itinerary she had mapped out for her honeymoon with Brad. But allowing Jared to escort her on a few of the more romantic adventures she'd organized was too bizarre to contemplate. She shook her head to dispel the tingly sensations causing her stomach to tighten. She mentally shook the erotic notions beginning to form, forcing her to come back to her current predicament.

"For all I know, my brother could be dead," she blurted.

Tears threatened. She shut her eyes to hold them back. No way would she break down in front of Jared.

"I'm sure he's okay." He reached over and patted her thigh.

Another sensual zing radiated straight up her mid-section and swelled throughout her body. More tense then before, she inwardly chastised herself for having such feelings when her brother could be lying in some unknown, shady location, dead or dying. Visions of him washed up on the beach made her shudder.

Jared parked the car, got out and circled around the front. He had her door opened before she had gathered her purse and reached for the handle. He took her hand, helped her out, then put his arm around her and led her through the parking lot into Rio's crowded old town. They strolled amid brightly painted tall buildings and narrow streets, and then rounded the corner of Rua Conçalves Dias. A tight, energized crowd filled the avenue. Dancers in skimpy, bright sequined costumes gyrated, mesmerizing bystanders. Those watching in awe clapped and swayed to the syncopated music coming from an equally colorful band that was set up close by. Further along the commons, several couples demonstrated the intricate steps of ballroom style samba as others went about their business as if they'd witness such goings-on on a daily basis. *Carnaval* was underway in the Old Town. Unable to resist the joviality of the music and dance, Marcia's tension slowly waned. She scanned the captivating landscape in front of her. She spotted a cluster of rough-looking men winding their way through the throng toward the other end of the street. They looked out of place among the merriment. From her vantage point, she could have sworn the man in the middle looked an awful lot like Russell. Her senses went on alert. Her instincts told her to run after them, to find out if it was her brother.

"Jared. Look. Down the street. I think I see Russell? Oh, my God. It's him. Come on. Hurry."

Before she could take a single step through the massive crowd to make a positive ID, the men were swallowed up by the milling pedestrians, and then disappeared around the corner and out of sight.

"They went around the end of the building. Come on. We've got to catch up to them."

"Are you sure it was Russell?" Jared rushed to keep up with her.

"I swear it was him. He was with two other men. Come on. We've got to catch up to them—make sure Russell is okay."

At least he was still alive.

Never leaving sight of the spot where Russell had disappeared, Marcia continued to pull on Jared's arm, tugging him along.

"Stay close, I'll get us through this crowd," Jared whispered in her ear, nudging her forward, his arm circled and wrapped snugly around her waist.

The music and colorful couple engrossed in the seductive samba in the center of the crowd didn't skip a beat as Jared shoved past them and ushered Marcia toward the end of the street. They rushed past the expansive windowed façade of the Confeiteria Colombo in all its glittery glory. Jared elbowed their way through the crowd, their progress stalled to a snail's pace, thanks to several bystanders engrossed in the festivities. Frustrated by the time they made it to the corner, Marcia was ready to tear her hair out. Russell was nowhere in sight.

"It was him. I know it was." She gasped for breath, clenching her hands at her side.

"I don't know what to say. I don't see a single lead at this point. Are you sure it was him?"

"Yes, I'm positive. We can't stop looking." She pleaded, scanning the dark intersection. "What if he's in danger? Needs our help? We can't stop searching."

His look told her he had her pegged for a nutcase. His hand holding hers tightened enough to make her think he understood. Maybe.

"Please," she pleaded again.

"We can circle the block, see if we can find him."

She threw her shaking body into his and hugged him.

"Thank you," she breathed against his safe, secure chest.

Her heart picked up a beat. She wanted to stay in his embrace a moment longer. She stepped back instead. She had to think of Russell, not the warmth of Jared's body crushed so close against hers. She tugged on his hand.

"Let's go."

Although the side streets weren't as crowded as the main avenue, there were plenty of revelers to slow their progress. Marcia had to admit defeat once they circled the block and arrived back at the café without spotting a single person that resembled Russell. Disappointed, they made their way back to the café.

The café's main floor was overcrowded. Tables and chairs were tightly woven around each other, and filled to capacity. The maître d' greeted and escorted them past the long mirrored bar on the left to the upstairs dining room. The table they were shown to overlooked the tearoom on the main floor below. Marcia's spirits were at war between succumbing to the beauty of the establishment and the vitality of *Carnaval,* and anxiety over her missing brother. Most likely in danger.

"While you were getting your things together at the

hotel, I called my office. My staff is checking Russell's contact list and schedule." Jared got right to the matter at hand. "As soon as they have something, they'll let me know. Whoever they are, they obviously want what they think Russell has in his possession. Any idea what they're looking for?"

His question sounded more like an accusation. Did he think she was keeping something from him?

"Not a clue." Marcia spread the linen napkin in her lap, keeping her eyes on Jared. "I haven't talked to Russell in a month. I didn't even know he was in Rio until his wife called and asked me to check in on him. Unless she's talked to him again and told him I was on my way to Rio, he doesn't even know I'm here."

Did Russell know she was in Rio? Had he gotten the message? Was it Russell with those men? If so, where were they going? She hadn't seen his face, so she had no idea whether or not it really was him. Was he with them under his own steam, or under duress?

"What is Russell really doing here in Rio? Why is he with those men?"

Marcia was interrupted when the waitress arrived with their wine. She poured a small portion in a glass for Jared to sample. He took a sip, nodded his head in approval. The waitress filled his glass, then poured hers, and placed the bottle in the silver wine bucket in the center of the table before she withdrew. Marcia took a sip of the fruity wine, welcoming the smooth, chilled liquid. Jared did the same and then hesitated while he set the glass on the table. The silence heavy, he raised his eyes to meet hers. He paused, his expression decisive. She wondered what went through his mind and what impact his assumptions would have on her.

Did he know why Russell was in Rio? Had he sent him?

"He's on assignment for the company," he answered. "We have several business contacts in South America who purchase our high-end avatar games. As our marketing rep, Russell was scheduled to meet with representatives from Argentina and Chile, as well as Brazil. We're in the process of expanding our business in South America and farther abroad—finding new outlets to market and sell our games."

"Do you think one of these reps trashed his room? What were they looking for? And why search my room?"

That's exactly what Jared wanted to know, too. Whoever had searched Russell's room had somehow made the connection linking him and Marcia. Dammit. Was she in danger? Was she in cahoots with Russell?

"And what about the Japanese?"

Shit. She knew about the Japanese. How deep was she involved?

"What about them?"

"Bea mentioned them—said Russell was supposed to meet with them."

Maybe he should be talking to Russell's wife to find out what he'd told her, instead of Marcia. If Marcia was in on the scheme with the Japanese, would she have mentioned it? Be asking about them? Did she really not know what Russell was up to? Were the men who'd trashed her room looking for the prototype of his latest avatar game?

"What did his wife tell you about the Japanese? Did she mention any names? A company?" Jared drummed his fingers on the table waiting for an answer.

What the hell was Russell up to?

"Nothing, other than he was to meet with the Brazilian representatives for a Japanese company out of Tokyo. When he called, he wasn't sure how long he would be in Rio. He told her he would call her after he met with them. Bea told me he seemed upset. She tried to talk him out of going, but he told her he needed to make these contacts. It was the only way he could clear his name. What does that mean? Why would he have to clear his name?"

"I'm not sure. But I'm going to find out what's going on. First, we have to find him."

Once again, their conversation was interrupted when the waitress served their meal. Jared was glad to see Marcia wasted no time picking up her fork and digging in. His own appetite had been nagging his stomach the last couple of hours. Despite the stress he'd been under lately, it didn't affect his enjoyment of sharing good food and being in the company of a beautiful woman. He'd often thought of Marcia over the past two years, usually when he'd been in conversation with her brother. Finding her walking the streets of Rio brought back feelings he'd been unable to suppress—still wanted to suppress, which was hard to do at the moment.

"Bea is expecting me to call her tonight. I can't tell her he's missing—she's under enough strain as it is with Heather. I don't know what this would do to her."

There had been talk about Russell's daughter's health issues—the house being close to foreclosure because of the high medical bills. If only Russell had come to him for help, he would gladly have given him a loan. Up until now, Russell had been a loyal, hardworking employee. He couldn't think of a single reason why he had turned against him, like this.

"Wait until tomorrow. I should have a report from my office by early afternoon. They might have news of his whereabouts. Everything will be cleared up and you'll have good news to share."

"I promised I'd call my sister after I arrived. I'll let her know what's going on—let her talk to Bea. She'll know what to say to her. Besides, I need to let them know how to contact me seeing as I'm not staying at the hotel."

"You can make the call as soon as we get to my brother's.

****

A black car screeched to a stop alongside the street, the rear door swung open, and a man stepped out and shoved Russell inside the vehicle. Before he could catch his balance, another assailant, already inside, yanked him further into the vehicle. As he attempted to adjust his body into a sitting position, a shooting pain shot down the back of his head. The worst headache he'd ever experienced radiated to his temples, his face, his neck. A bright light flashed in front of his eyes. He slumped forward, and blacked out.

Russell woke to severe throbbing radiating down the back of his brain. He reached behind his head to find the cause of the pain only to have his right hand yanked back in place. A sharp twinge circled his wrist. With blurred vision, he looked over to find his hand cuffed to the springs of an old, rusted metal bed. He checked his left hand, relieved to find it free. This time, he was able to slowly raise his hand, which connected with a lump the size of a golf ball at the base of his neck. And then, he remembered. He lay back on the thin mattress, smelling of mildew and stale urine, and void of a pillow. He took a deep breath, and wished he hadn't—the stench made his stomach lurch.

Ricardo and Paul had been waiting for him, pacing in front of Confeiteria Colombo. He'd been ten minutes late, thanks to the horrific traffic and his quick stop at the post office. They hadn't been happy. Instead of going inside, they immediately surrounded him, grabbed his arms, and ushered him into the energetic crowd. They'd each jabbed a gun into either side of his ribcage. It would have been useless to kick up a fuss.

"We will shoot you where you walk if you make a commotion. We have silencers and people will think you are drunk on *Carnaval*." Ricardo had warned as he wiggled the gun in his face. "Cooperate, and you live another day."

With the music, dancing, and general high spirits of the packed street, Russell was sure no one else had heard, or had paid them any attention. He hadn't wanted to provoke them—Paul was right, he wanted to live another day. Wanted to see his family again.

He sat up and swung his legs over the side of the bed. His head buzzed, his stomach lurched, he swallowed back the bile threatening to dislodge. The room was dark, musty, and damp. The little bit of light shining through the dirty window near the ceiling seemed to be coming from a yellowed lamplight right outside the building. Not sure how long he'd been out cold, he could tell it was obviously nighttime. Adjusting his eyesight, he searched his surroundings for an escape route. There didn't seem to be one.

Russell lay back on the lumpy mattress, more than

likely inhabited with bedbugs. A plume of dust shot into the air smelling of old sweat. He closed his eyes, powerless. "Dear Lord, help me get out of this alive," he prayed. "I need to be there for Bea and Heather."

The metal door slammed open. Russell jerked upright, his arm yanked back, holding him place. He closed his eyes to stop the dizzy spell that hit once again. When he opened them, two men he hadn't seen before approached.

"So, you are awake. We will get answers for Mr. Osaka, then we will see what will become of you."

The second man approached more slowly, a thin wooden club clenched menacingly in his fat fist. Russell wasn't sure how many more blows to the head he could handle, but he didn't have a choice. He didn't have any information for these thugs.

"We have searched your room for the prototype and did not find it. Did you sell it to another dealer for more money? Are you playing Mr. Osaka for a fool? You think to up the ante? It will not work."

The man stepped closer. The thug with the club followed suit. Russell remained motionless, not sure what to expect. He hadn't envisioned this scenario when he mailed the fake prototype back to Jared. From the looks of the two men, it wouldn't have made any difference if he handed it over to them or not—he was a dead man. It was only a matter of time.

"Now, you will tell us where the prototype is, or my friend here will be forced to entice you to talk. You understand?"

"I have nothing to tell you. I don't have the prototype. I didn't sell it to anyone. I am here only to find out who is selling them to Mr. Osaka."

"A likely story. Mr. Osaka does not like double-crossers. He wants the prototype as promised by Mr. Rose."

"I don't know a Mr. Rose. There is no one at the company with that name." He had an idea who it was, but there was no concrete evidence yet. He'd informed Jared in the note he'd sent, asking him to check it out.

"Come now. Mr. Rose works for Reed Technologies. You must know him."

If he was right about who this Mr. Rose was, the next question was, why was he using him as a scapegoat—blaming him for selling out Jared's business? The man must be close to being discovered if he needed to put the blame on an innocent bystander.

"You should check with your original contact."

"Give a care with your tone. My comrade is very handy with persuasion."

The man with the club stepped forward. Russell wasn't ready for the sharp slap of the stick against his knee. The contact excruciating—the yelp automatic. As he rubbed his knee with his free hand, the heavyset man tapped his wrist in warning. This time Russell kept silent, the pain fluctuating between knee and wrist. He lay back again, held his breath hoping it would ease the pain.

"Again, I ask—where is the prototype?"

Russell swallowed. "I don't know."

"Does your sister, Miss Marcia, have it? Have you given it to her for safekeeping?"

"Marcia?" Russell jerked upright. How did they find out Marcia was his sister? "What about Marcia?"

"Ah, she left you a message on your phone. We listened to it when we searched your room. Said she was on her way to Rio to help you. It was kind of her to give us her hotel address in Rio. Unfortunately, we found nothing in her room. Tell me, is she the Rose?"

Russell's stomach cringed. Never one to want to inflict pain on anyone, he had the strongest urge to do bodily damage to the men who were in control of not only his life, but his sister's as well. God forbid. Had they threaten Bea or Heather, too?

"*No!* She has nothing to do with Reed Technologies. She happens to be here on her honeymoon. I told you, I don't know this Mr. Rose. But it is not my sister."

"Well, if she is on her honeymoon, as you claim, where is her new husband? There was no sign of another person in her room. No man waiting with open arms to receive his new bride. I think you are trying to throw us off track. I think she is the Rose and you are trying to hide the truth from us."

"I tell you, she is not the Rose."

"We do not have much time, but I assure you, you will tell us."

Once again the heavyset monster swung his club with such force at Russell's head—the hard blow knocked him back on the cold, dirty mattress. And once again, darkness followed.

Chapter Five

Jared hadn't asked for any of this. Following in his family's footsteps, starting his own technology business seemed a natural progression of his childhood. Who hadn't loved playing all those dynamic interactive games as a kid? But he had also loved living on his grandfather's ranch. In fact, he loved it so much he'd bought into it right after college. With his grandparents gone, he was the sole owner of one of the biggest spreads in Northeastern Oregon. Thankfully, he had Cash, his head wrangler, to manage the Double R while he concentrated on Reed Technologies' problems.

With the help of his long-time classmate and friend, Hank, the tech company had taken off like wildfire. It had grown so fast he'd hardly been able to keep up. He had hired two new young men fresh out of college to help out with the technical and design aspect of the business, and had hired Russell Kline as his marketing rep. But the last couple of years sales had dwindled. Other companies were coming out with games similar to his, and his sales declined. He'd made a gigantic effort to keep Reed Technologies separate from the Double R. Borrowing money from one to support the other was simply not good business. Learning one of his best employees was selling him out undermined his confidence in believing he was a good judge of character. Russell, a supportive, religious family man had seemed above board—up front, honest, and willing to go that extra mile. No way had he ever imagined the man would be the one to stab him in the back. But the proof Hank had produced said otherwise.

He snuck a peek at Marcia sitting next to him in the car as he drove down the strip toward his brother's neighborhood. Her head lolled against the headrest. The on-coming traffic lights highlighted her pale, fatigued features. Was she involved with her brother's scheme? God he hoped not. She'd appeared to be genuinely upset and concerned when she discovered her brother's room had been ransacked. She'd been shocked and so distraught when she walked in and found her own room had been tipped upside down. And Lord help him, she'd felt so good in his arms when she'd all but collapsed and he caught her outside her brother's hotel. It was all he could do not to draw her closer and sink his lips into hers.

But once again, his business trumped his love life—such as it was at the moment. He needed to figure out what the hell was going on—who was selling his avatar games before they could be marketed. Who better to sell to the highest bidder than his marketing rep—Russell? The documents Hank had shown him were proof positive evidence against Russell.

Jared turned off the main highway along the beach front into the Barra de Tijuca district. He'd been surprised his brother had settled in this up-and-coming neighborhood which was starting to rival the main district of Rio. But the suburbs were well-groomed. Kurt's home was hidden behind extensive gardens, giving it a secluded appearance. He knew Kurt's wife took great pleasure in tending her flowerbeds. He passed through an open gate, up a drive bordered with various shrubs in bloom, and stopped in front of the entrance of a Spanish-style home.

"We're here." He hated to wake her, she looked so peaceful.

Marcia stirred when he hit the brakes and shut the motor off. She stretched and gazed out the window.

"Where is here?" Marcia yawned and rubbed her eyes.

A tug yanked at his heart. Even disheveled she was a beautiful woman. It was getting harder and harder to ignore these unwelcomed feelings whenever she was in the same time zone.

"Come on. Let's get you inside so you can get some sleep. I called ahead. Sophia promised to have our rooms ready when we arrived. We can deal with everything else tomorrow."

"I really should call my sister. Let her know what's going on. Bea must be going crazy waiting to find out if I've made contact with Russell."

"Get settled, then you can make your call."

Kurt's wife, Sophia, met them at the front door. A petite woman with a mass of long unruly auburn hair, she wore black slacks and a mint green silk tank top. Marcia had no trouble figuring out why Jared's brother had married her—she was a beautiful, sexy woman who bubbled over with energy.

"We have been waiting for you." Sophia welcomed them, then stepped forward, stood on her tip-toes, and gave Jared a big hug—difficult, as she was head and shoulders shorter.

Jared lifted her off the porch and gave her a gentle squeeze, then placed a brief kiss on her forehead.

"Good to see you, too."

He set Sophia down, and then drew Marcia forward.

"Sophia, this is Marcia Kline. Marcia, my sister-in-law, Sophia."

"Pleased to finally see Jared bring his girl to meet us." She beamed up at Jared, and then urged them both inside.

"Oh, but I'm not…"

"Come. Come. Kurt is waiting for us in the library." Sophia brushed Marcia's words aside. "He is anxious to meet you, too. Jared, you stay away too long and work much too hard. You need to visit us more often."

"It works both ways, Sophia. You and Kurt need to come for a visit at the ranch."

"Well, it has been a long time. You know how your brother feels about the ranch. Such sad memories. He has his own computer business here in Rio. He uses it to help the underprivileged."

The entranceway was spacious, uncluttered. An oblong wooden table took up most of the wall space to the left, a large ornate gold framed mirror hung directly above, and a vase of vibrant pink *Cattleya labiata*, also known as the Queen of the Orchids in Brazil, contrasted with the dark wood. A long multi-colored carpeted runner led to a staircase next to open French style double doors where Sophia guided them. Marcia walked into the library and recognized Kurt immediately. She'd met him at Jared's ranch two years ago, and still couldn't get over how much he looked like Jared—only a shorter version.

"It's good to see you again, Marcia." His

handshake was firm.

He stepped back and offered his hand to Jared. "And you, big brother. It's about time you paid us a visit."

She wasn't surprised to see Jared initiate a playful embrace. The camaraderie between the two brothers had been evident during her time at the Double R's barbecue.

"Is he treating you right, Sophia? Not spending too much time on his computer classes?" Jared smiled.

"We compromise. He teaches the children the techniques in computer. I teach them the skill of *dança*. You will come to this year's exhibition while you are here. After all, it is *Carnaval*. My group will be showing off what they have learned at the local hall. We are not big enough for the major shows, or the competition."

"Sophia is a samba instructor and has played a big part in keeping the locals off the streets by holding classes in the evening," Kurt told her.

"Perhaps I teach you while you are here? You can *dança* with Jared. He is a good dancer, thanks to my instruction."

"Don't go there, Sophia," Jared warned. "You know I'm not a great dancer."

"Don't let him fool you. He can teach you better. I am surprised he has not shared his talent with you already."

"Kurt works with the poorer children, teaching computer skills so they can get work instead of wandering the streets and becoming *bandidos* when they finish school," Jared interjected, effectively changing the topic of conversation.

"Sophie, why don't you show our guest to her room, she looks done in." Kurt apparently was also ready to change the topic.

"Of course. My pleasure. Come. Your room is this way waiting for you."

"Meet me back here when you're ready," Jared called as she and Sophia climbed the stairs. "You can use the phone in the library to call home."

"Come, Marcia. I have put you in the room next to Jared."

Marcia didn't like the gleam in Sophia's eyes, nor the smile on her face. It was obvious what was on her mind.

"Sophia, I don't want you and Kurt to get the wrong impression about me and Jared. We don't have a relationship. In fact, I haven't seen him in two years. We happened to cross paths today by accident."

"Ah, but it is kismet you two meet again. Kurt says the two of you had a 'thing' a while ago. Yes?"

"It was nothing. Really. In fact, I was recently engaged to someone else."

Marcia had had enough of matchmakers. She didn't need another one messing up her life. Jared had made it very clear when last they met. Her track record wasn't a stellar one, and honestly, she needed to concentrate on finding her brother, not getting involved in another relationship that was going nowhere.

"It is small, but you will be *confortável*." Sophia swung the door wide for Marcia to enter the bedroom. "When you come down we will have coffee and talk about this engagement. Jared tells me it is broken and you are here alone."

What else had Jared told his brother and sister-in-law about her? Did they know about Russell?

A wrought-iron double bed, draped in a fluffy, pastel melon-colored down coverlet with matching pillows, took up the center of the room. Marcia was ready to sink into it and forget about her disastrous day.

"This is lovely. Thanks for letting me stay on such short notice."

"You are most welcome." Sophia smiled, and then pointed across the spacious room. "There is a private *banheiro* to the left of the window where you can freshen up. I apologize, I assumed you and Jared were together—his room is through the connecting door to the right. Jared is a *respeitável* man. You will have no *dificuldades* from him."

Again, Sophia didn't look at all apologetic. Smug was a better word. And as for Jared, well…he really was a respectable man.

"I will give you time alone while you settle," Sophia continued. "Then, we have *café* on the *pátio*. We enjoy the coolness of *á noite*. Relax."

Marcia freshened up, and then made her way back down to the library. Jared and Kurt rose from wing-backed chairs situated around a circular coffee table in the center of the room. Again, Marcia was struck by the family resemblance between the two men—strong handsome genes despite their differences.

"We will leave you to make your call." Kurt indicated the phone on the library table on the far side of the room. "The patio is through those doors when you're ready. I understand Sophie has coffee underway."

"I'll be outside if you need me." Jared moved toward the glass-sliding doors. "Take your time."

His concerned look tugged at her heart. Did he know how hard this call was going to be?

"Thank you both. I'll be fine."

Poor Bea. There was nothing to do but wait for news of Russell. And the news of Russell was not good. Thankfully, she had decided to call Sammie instead of her sister-in-law.

But what could she say to her sister? Waking her up this early in the morning back in the States was going to be upsetting enough. Telling her their brother was missing, possibly dragged off by a couple of thugs was going to put her in panic mode. Thankfully, Sammie's husband, Mark, would be there for moral support. She hoped her sister answered the phone before it clicked on to the answering machine. This was not the kind of message to leave hanging.

Marcia's heart sank as the machine clicked on. About to hang up, Sammie's sleepy voice answered.

"Sammie? It's Marcia. I'm so sorry to wake you, but I have some disturbing news about Russell."

"What? Give me a minute. What time is it?"

Papers rustled, a lamp was clicked on, and Sammie moaned on the other end of the line.

"I'm sorry to call you so early, but I wanted to catch you before you left the house."

"It's Russell, isn't it? Oh, my, God. What happened?"

"I don't know. I left a message—asked him to meet me at the airport. Apparently he never got it, because he never showed up. I tried calling him when I got to my hotel. He didn't answer his phone. I left another message, but he still hasn't returned my call. I went to his hotel room and found someone had ransacked it."

"What? Where's Russell now?"

"I don't know. Bea asked me to call her, but there is no way I can tell her any of this. You know how it would affect her. Can you call her for me? Tell her I arrived safely and as soon as I get settled and connect with Russell I'll be in touch?"

She wasn't about to tell her sister that someone had broken into her room as well. And Sammie didn't need to know she was staying with Jared and his brother. She had cried on Sammie's shoulder when she'd come back from Jared's ranch two years ago. Sammie was well aware of the short disastrous relationship with Jared. She would make too much of their current situation and chance meeting. Her sister was a lot like Sophia.

"Did you report him missing? What are the police doing about it?"

Marcia didn't want to tell her sister the police weren't overly concerned.

"It's *Carnaval.* They are swamped at the moment trying to keep order."

"I'll call Bradley—have him put his people on this right away. Something sounds awfully fishy with Jared and his company."

"*NO!* Whatever you do, do not contact Brad. If you have to, call a different P.I. firm."

"Sorry, but you know his company is the best. He'll get to the bottom of this whole fiasco and find Russell before you know it."

"Sammie. *Do. Not. Call. Brad.*"

"You are alone in Rio. Do you know anyone there who can help you?"

She didn't know a single sole in Rio de Janeiro, other than Jared and his family. She wasn't ready to let her sister know they were outside the door waiting for her on the patio. But she didn't want her sister to worry about her being in Rio alone. She took a deep breath, held it, then let it out slowly.

"I met Jared Reed today. If I ask him, I'm sure he'll help me."

"Can you trust him? After all, he's Russell's employer. Something isn't right with the company. We need someone outside Reed Technologies—someone impartial."

"You know what Brad will think. And right now I do not want to look into his cheating face, let alone be indebted to him for helping us."

"He owes you. Give me the details, and I'll have Mark pass them along. You won't even have to speak to the pervert."

Not happy with the current situation in Rio, and especially with Sammie wanting to contact Brad, Marcia filled Sammie in on what had happened since arriving in Rio. She left out her own hotel room break-in, and the fact that she was staying with the Reeds.

"Give me a number where we can contact you. I'll call as soon as I hear back from Brad."

Marcia gave Sammie the information and hung up, then made her way out to the patio. The evening was warm—the surrounding gardens were a tropical paradise. A string of solar torches lined the walk and a small lily pond had a trickling waterfall in the center. The smell of coffee teased her senses back to the present.

All three looked at her expectantly. She sat in the only cushioned chair available—next to Jared.

"How did it go?"

Marcia looked at Jared's brother and sister-in-law, then back at Jared, not sure what to say in front of them. No way could she tell Jared his company was about to be investigated by her ex-fiancé. She was becoming bogged down keeping secrets.

"Fine. My sister is handling it." She sat next to him, flicked a wisp of hair that had come loose behind her ear, and wrung her hands in her lap.

"Jared told us about your brother. I am sorry." Sophia pouted her lips, then smiled. "Tomorrow is Sunday. We will go to special services at Cristo Redentor in the morning. We will ask for help to find your brother. Tonight we will enjoy our *café*. Perhaps Jared will give you a stroll through our gardens before you call it a night. They are lovely in the moonlight."

She didn't want to offend Sophia, but no way was she about to go for a stroll with Jared—moonlight or no moonlight.

Chapter Six

Strolling in the gardens with Jared the night before hadn't been productive. They spoke briefly of her conversation with Sammie. If he thought she held something back, he gave no indication. He didn't pry for answers she didn't want to give. Too exhausted to worry about his problems one way or another, she had begged off extending their walk. He'd been a perfect gentleman and let her escape with a casual goodnight once they retraced their steps back to the patio.

After a sleepless night, she hoped attending the services at Cristo Redentor—Christ the Redeemer—would help get her out of her funk. Visiting the monolithic statue was something she had looked forward to when she'd planned her honeymoon. Attending services hadn't been on her radar, but she looked forward to the experience. After being attacked and her room ransacked, going with Jared and his family instead of going alone was comforting.

Swirls of heavy fog had set in along the coastline and obliterated both Sugar Loaf and Christ the Redeemer. Despite the early morning mist, it was a warm start to the day. It was bound to get hotter as the sun's penetration drew the fog up and away. Dressed in a sleeveless cotton dress of periwinkle blue, she'd flung her matching floral silk scarf over her shoulders to cover her head and shoulders during the service. Her hair tucked snugly into a French twist, she let her bangs swing sideways over her left brow.

The ride to Corcovado Hill and Christ the Redeemer was anything but quiet. Sophia chatted the entire way.

"You will love it. Such magnificent views. Even I do not tire of it. And for you, we will take the cog train from Cosme Velho. Then up the steep escalator to the top. Ah. They have a small outdoor café. We will get a coffee and pastry. The fog—it will disappear like magic. You will see. You will love it. I tell you, there is nothing like it—so romantic. Am I right, Kurt? It will be a splendid day."

Kurt smiled at his wife, an endearing look on his face. He was truly in love with her. Marcia smiled at Jared, expecting a humorous look in reaction to Sophia's monologue. But Jared spent the ride looking out the window, ignoring her.

"I appreciate you including me in your outing today," she told Sophia. "I'm sure I will enjoy every minute of it."

Despite her brother's disappearance, the fact that she was in Rio, and in such dynamic company, helped to alleviate some of her anxiety—Sophia's enthusiasm contagious.

By the time they arrived at the top of the stone summit and settled in around the roped-off area, the service began. Other locals, as well as tourists, flowed in, jostling for a place to stand close to the service. People in all forms of dress swarmed in groups, or individually. Before long they were all standing facing the statue, elbow to elbow. Despite the religious beliefs of those in attendance, all were intent on the Catholic

Mass in progress. Papal servants dressed in white robes and gold headdresses, handled gold chalices, staphs, and bells with ceremony.

Craning her neck, Marcia was able to see a portion of Christ the Redeemer from above the knees up to the outline of the outstretched arms.

"Wait until the fog lifts completely," Jared whispered in her ear. "It's a sight you'll remember forever."

He was right. By the time the service was half over, the sun had dried the haze off the earth and Christ the Redeemer looked down on those assembled, arms outstretched, as if it was part of the service. But what made it even more memorable? She stood beside Jared, and he had his arm around her shoulders. She smiled. When he smiled back down at her it was as if they were the only two standing on the mountain top.

So intent on the service, and the warmth emanating from Jared's arm circling her shoulders, Marcia was jolted back to reality as two men nudged against her, causing her to move away from Jared. His arms dropped as they shuffled to make room for the newcomers. Not wanting to be rude, she inched her way toward Sophia and Kurt.

Concentrating on the service once again, Marcia was surprised to find Kurt and Sophia, as well as Jared, no longer close by. She searched frantically for Jared, and found him searching the area for her. She waved, caught his attention, and relaxed at the relieved look on his face. About to make her way toward him, his smile turned upside down. Before she could figure out what had him upset, two men grabbed her arm, swung her around, and forced her through the crowd in the opposite direction.

"Do not speak in alarm. We will have no choice but to use these knives close to your ribs. Do you understand?"

"What do you want? Where is my brother? What have you done with him?" Marcia shoved the men aside only to feel the sharp sting of a blade as it dug through her dress. Thankfully, the scarf was also in the way and kept the tip from slicing her skin.

"Quiet. Do not be foolish. You give us what we want and we will let you go. But now, you come with us. *Rapidamente*—quickly."

Were these the same men who had attacked her near Russell's hotel? Where was Jared? She couldn't see him through the crowd milling about.

Marcia was out of breath by the time they reached the escalator, and nearly tripping over her own feet. Not waiting for the motorized stairs to carry them down, her captors dragged her toward a narrow set of stairs. Not able to keep up with them, they lifted her off her feet and flew down the steep flight toward the bottom. Once on solid ground they carried her toward the parking area. Wanting to call out to Jared, she twisted her head to see if anyone was paying any attention to the odd spectacle they had to be making.

"Do not make a scene. There is no one close by to care, I assure you."

"You have got to be kidding. Someone cares. Jared cares. He is probably right behind us."

Where the hell was he, anyway?

They dragged her toward a small black car. If she was pushed inside, Jared would never find her—like they weren't able to find Russell. She couldn't chance it. She would end up dead somewhere—somewhere where no one would ever find her. Or worse, be unable to identify her if they did find her. Her mind raced at the images she'd conjured up.

Her feet on the ground, she made a fast decision to stop walking—making it more difficult for them to drag her any further. The knife sliced into her skin on her left side as she fell forward.

The two men tripped over their own feet as she tumbled to the pavement. She rolled to the side, and did a low backward somersault, her cheerleading and aerobic skills kicking in. The two men landed face down on the hard pavement with a loud grunt. Portuguese words Marcia was sure were obscene followed as she made her escape. She had to get away, blend into the crowd so they couldn't find her—get at her. She didn't get far however, when two strong arms snatched her from the crowd.

"Holy shit, where did you learn how to perform such a stunt like that—and in a dress?" Jared managed between deep breaths next to her ears. "You had the whole crowd mesmerized."

"Cheerleading. Some things you never forget."

She scanned the crowd. Sure enough, everyone was gawking at her. She brushed the stray tendrils that had come loose behind her ears. Jared took her in his protective arms and held her in such a tight grip she couldn't breathe. She wrapped her arms around him and held on despite the pain in her side.

"Get me out of here before they come after Kurt and Sophia, too. They aren't involved in any of this—whatever 'this' is."

Jared reluctantly removed his arms from around

her shaking shoulders. His hands rested on her waist. She flinched, but didn't cry out.

"What is it? What's wrong?"

"Their knife cut my dress and punctured my skin. Come on, hurry, let's get out of here."

"Not so fast. Let me take a look." Jared raised her arm and brushed her scarf aside, and drew in a deep breath. The dress was cut wide and Jared could see the injury was much more than a scratch. A large circle of blood stained the side of her dress. They might not have caused damage the first time they attacked her, but this time was different. They'd managed to break the skin, and dig deep.

"We need to get your injury looked at right away." He lifted the scarf from around her neck and folded it into a square. "Put this on it, hold tight. It will stop the blood flow. Do you think you can manage until we get down off the hill?"

"I'm not going to faint on you if that's what you're worried about. I'm more concerned those two thugs will go after Kurt and Sophia if they see me with them. Do you think they're gone?"

"They picked themselves up and dove into their vehicle and took off like the bullet I wished I had along with a gun so I could shoot them."

"Do you mind if we sit down for a few minutes?"

"Not a problem. We'll wait for Kurt and Sophia at the *café* where we planned to meet after the services."

"I could use a stiff drink right about now. Something with ice in it."

"You got it."

He kept his arm around her as they slowly made their way back up the escalator to the café. Kurt and

Sophia were already seated, sipping a coffee.

"Oh! What is wrong?" Sophia ran to her side. "You don't look so good. Did something happen? We wondered where the two of you got off to, didn't we Kurt?"

"Marcia was accosted by two men. They were trying to abduct her. She's bleeding. We need some ice and a clean cloth."

"A small cut, I will be fine."

"Oh, my goodness. I will get ice. You stay here. Sit." Sophia rushed toward the café counter.

Kurt waited until his wife left the table. "What the hell is going on?"

Jared helped Marcia to sit, careful not to jar her ribs. Once she was settled, he sat next to his brother. Before he had a chance to respond, not only was Sophia back with ice, but a waitress was carrying a tray of steaming coffee to their table.

"Here. You put this ice on to stop the flow of blood. Give me your scarf. I will wrap it around like a bandage so you can free your hands to enjoy your coffee. They will arrive with pastries in a moment."

While Sophia assisted Marcia, Jared took the opportunity to fill Kurt in as to the events that had just taken place. He had to admit trying to keep things under wraps from Sophia wasn't working. Sophia settled into her seat, and then leaned into their conversation.

"So you suspect her brother has been kidnapped? He is in danger? Do they think your Marcia is involved?"

"Sophia, don't jump to conclusions." Kurt's effort to calm his wife was in vain. "This could have been a simple misunderstanding. You know how crazy

Carnaval can be."

"Don't I know it? Oh, Marcia, you have come at a special, crazy time of year. Of course, you never know what goes on during *Carnaval*. Kurt, we should take Jared and Marcia to the club. Let them see the fantastic dance routines my girls can do. They can try their hand at some of the *samba pagode*." She turned to Marcia. "It is like *samba de gafieira* only without the acrobatic steps. I will teach you. It is a combination of a waltz and a tango. So romantic," Sophia said in a dramatic swoon.

"Sophia, I'm not sure it's a good idea," Kurt interjected, putting his hands on his hips.

"It is perfect time. Get their mind off their troubles. It is what *Carnaval* is all about? Oh, you will love it, Marcia. I will make the arrangements. We will go to the *Plataforma* show—you will see. Then we will have our own private dance class." Sophia clapped her hands, took a satisfied breath and sipped her coffee.

Kurt hung his head and shook it. "There is no stopping her, I'm afraid. I am sorry."

Jared was relieved to see the smile on Marcia's face, as well as the color return to her flushed cheeks. Sophia did have that effect on people. It was one of the things about her his brother loved, despite his apology.

Sophia's head bobbed up before anyone could fill in the half-space of quiet. She sipped from her demitasse cup, swallowed the thick concoction, and then announced her next decision.

"We will call and make reservations at Porcao for dinner first. Have you ever been to such a restaurant before?"

Jared caught Marcia's startled look, also an effect

Sophia had on people.

"Sophia, you are like a steam roller," Kurt chided, shaking his head. "Give Marcia a chance to deal with the latest episode. Drink your coffee so we can take her to get medical attention."

"You two stay. I'll call a taxi and get Marcia to the hospital." Jared stood and dashed around the table to help Marcia. "We'll meet you back at the house. Then, if she feels up to it, we can go to Porcao's for dinner later tonight."

"I don't mean to be a bother." Marcia stood before Jared reached her side. "Really, Jared. This cut isn't severe enough to require attention. In fact, it's stopped bleeding and doesn't hurt at all."

"Don't argue. It needs looking after."

"You take the car. We will call a taxi." Kurt put his coffee cup on the table and looked to Sophia for confirmation. "It will save time. We'll see you back at the house."

Once in the privacy of the trolley-type cog train, going down the hill to their parked car, Marcia faced Jared. She wanted answers.

"Okay, Jared Reed. What's going on? Why are these men after me? Why do they think I have your prototypes? And why is it so important that they have to snatch me, of all people? Obviously, they've been following me since I got to Rio."

"Wait until we get to the car where we can talk in private."

The trip down off Corcovado Hill took an eternity. The view, on the other hand, took her breath away. The bright tropical sun shone over the city of Rio in an exotic, romantic panoramic view. Across the cerulean ocean stood Sugar Loaf Mountain, jutting majestically like someone had plunked it there for touristy effect. A moment of melancholy washed over her—she should be experiencing this in wedded bliss. Instead, she was single, alone, and being stalked. Where was the fun in that?

Jared stayed by her side, scanning the area as they exited the cog train and walked to the car. Once inside the vehicle, he faced her. She held her breath, waiting. He shook his head, looked out the window, and then back at her again.

"Honestly, I have no idea what to think—no idea how they learned of your connection to Russell. Are you sure you don't have a disk, a flash drive, anything Russell might have slipped to you?"

"I told you, I haven't seen Russell since I arrived. He didn't know I was coming."

"He didn't know you were coming to Rio for your honeymoon?"

"Well, I called from New York to let him know I was coming alone, and would he meet me at the airport. But I never talked to him. He never answered, so I left a message. When I arrived at the airport, he never showed. I had to catch a taxi to my hotel. Do you think they checked Russell's calls? Found out where I had reservations?"

"Possibly. It might explain how they knew where you were staying."

He didn't sound as if he believed her.

"Russell is not the one selling your games. He doesn't have a criminal bone in his body. He's been set up. Framed. Someone else in your company must be selling you out. Someone in the design department? Did your informant check out anyone else? Someone who might have a gripe with you or your company? Maybe someone on the ranch? Someone with ties to Rio?"

"I keep things separate when it comes to the Double R and Reed Technologies. I've had no problems with any of my employees or the wranglers."

He was well liked by all his employees. He had included all of them from both his tech company and the ranch and their families at the barbecue she'd attended. Everyone she had spoken to talked highly of him as an employer. He was friendly and on a first-name basis with everyone including the children. She rubbed her ribs and sank back in her seat.

"Sorry. Let's get you taken care. I'll check in with the police to see if they have any word about your brother—let them know about this incident. We'll take it from there."

She only hoped they found Russell so he could set the record straight.

Chapter Seven

Not needing anything other than a secure bandage and an antibiotic, Marcia was released from the emergency room. Jared met her in the waiting area.

"I'm fine. No stitches."

"Great. Let's go. I called and reported the incident while you were being seen."

"What did they say?"

He hesitated. She had her answer.

"It's *Carnaval*. They will keep an open eye."

"Of course."

"I also called Kurt and Sophia. They made reservations at the restaurant for later tonight. We have time to stop for a light snack, then walk along the beach and relax, if you're up to it."

"Sounds wonderful. Thanks. Afterwards, I'd like to stop back at the hotel to see if there are any messages."

They found a parking place close to the hotel, and walked to the nearest outdoor café where they found an empty seat, among the varied tourists. Jared ordered a local beer, and Marcia chose a piña colada. The cool fruity drink quenched her thirst. The café was crowded, noisy, and the music blared overhead making talk impossible. It was just as well. Marcia's mind reeled from the events to date, and she wondered what had become of Russell.

They ordered burgers and fries. When the last fry

was dealt with, Jared paid the bill and the two of them made their way across the street to the beach.

"Kick off your shoes and enjoy the water."

Marcia didn't hesitate. She'd been longing to sink her toes in the sand and water again. Jared did the same, and after arranging his shoes in his left hand, he took her free hand and rubbed his thumb over her wrist. For some reason, being with him gave her a sense of wellbeing. Protected. Especially after the last few incidents. It was a comfort. The warmth of her hand in his, and the tropical breeze brushing her face acted as a balm to her tattered self-esteem. The coolness of the ocean against her feet grounded her.

They strolled and splashed in the water in companionable silence along the shoreline. Sugar Loaf Mountain towered across the bay. They had walked a fair distance when Jared tugged on her hand, forcing her to a stop beside him. Her bare arm brushed against his, and a warmth which had nothing to do with the hot afternoon sun infused her. She had the strongest urge to lean into him, rest her head against his chest. He gazed down into her eyes. Her entire body melted with the concern and caring reflected in his eyes. She hadn't expected this from Jared. He was out to prove her brother intended to sell his prototypes to the Japanese, and assumed she was in cahoots with Russell. But here he was, almost making love to her with his look—his touch.

"We should head back. Have a chance to relax and get ready for dinner tonight. Maybe you should lie down and rest."

The tone of his voice was abrupt. She stepped back. Dropped her hand to her side. Had it been her imagination—wishful thinking on her part that he cared?

"I am ready to fall asleep. Walking the beach was too relaxing. Thanks for taking the time to be with me."

"You've been through a lot in the short time you've been in Rio. You needed to unwind. Believe me, after eating dinner at Porcao's tonight, you'll get a good night's sleep."

"I'd sleep better if I knew Russell was safe."

"We'll find him. Kurt's checking with his connections in the *barrio*. Working with the underprivileged has afforded him a few contacts who appreciate what he's doing to help the kids get out of the slums and gain experience to help them find employment later on in life. One of them might have gotten wind of something and be willing to offer information."

"Thanks. I know you think Russell is trying to sell your prototype, but I know he isn't."

They headed back down the beach toward the hotel.

"The evidence proves otherwise."

"What evidence?"

"Bank statements, other documents my company's P.I. was able to uncover. It seems your brother's financial difficulties were mysteriously taken care of, as well as an unexplained nest egg which appeared in his accounts."

"Unexplained? Did you even think to ask him where the money came from? Why he needed the money?"

"I've discovered it was mostly needed for medical expenses. But I've only recently found out about it.

Like you, I haven't had a chance to talk to him. I'm trying to get to the bottom of this, and came to Rio so I could."

"For your information, Russell and Bea's church held a fund-raiser to help them with Heather's medical expenses they've racked up the last three years. They've spent every cent they could get their hands on to cover the many hospital visits, the tests, the blood transfusions. Apparently, the insurance coverage wasn't adequate enough to cover it. They were about to lose everything, including their home. It just so happened that someone gave an anonymous, generous donation. It covered all their expenses with enough to help pay off the mortgage on the house, and have money for future expenses. And, a college education for Heather."

"I didn't know."

His low voice and tight lips confirmed it. He hadn't been made aware of Russell's dire needs. Or the fact that the church had held a benefit for the family.

"It wasn't in the report your people prepared?"

"If it was, I wasn't informed."

"Maybe you'd better double-check. Russell has no reason to sell your games. Maybe you should seriously look at someone else in your company. Someone either in need of a large amount of money, or someone with a grudge."

"I can't think of a single person with a grudge. I'm sure Hank would have kept me informed it there was a problem. He knows I like to deal with situations when they arise so they don't fester and cause problems."

"What about the ranch? Maybe someone on the Double R isn't happy."

"Cash keeps me informed about ranch matters. He

hasn't said a word."

"Does someone have a miff with Russell? An axe to grind? Someone capable of using him to cover their own behind?"

"Not that I'm aware of."

Marcia didn't mention that Sammie had enlisted her ex-fiancé to investigate Jared's company's affairs. She hadn't wanted Brad to be the one to do it, but to be honest, Brad was an excellent P.I. And, darn it, something wasn't adding up. Someone needed to check it out—someone able to be objective and get the specifics straight before something terrible happened to Russell. If it hadn't already.

They crossed the street to the hotel, and then made their way to the concierge at the front desk.

"Are there any messages for Miss Kline—Marcia Kline?" Jared leaned against the counter and tapped his fingers on the polished surface.

The tall Brazilian checked behind the counter, and retrieved two envelopes.

"Yes. There are two for Miss Kline." He handed them to Jared, a smile on his handsome face directed her way.

Jared passed them to Marcia. She read the first one. And froze.

"What?" Jared reached for the paper. "Let me see it."

Marcia handed it to him. "They think I have the prototype and insist I hand it over to them—or they'll kill Russell. Oh, my, God, Jared. What am I going to do? I don't have it. I can't give them something I don't have." Her world was falling apart around her. Tears filled her eyes.

She waited while Jared read the note.

"Who is Mr. Rose?" He lifted his eyebrows and scowled.

"How should I know? It's your company. Don't you know?"

"I have no idea. The name doesn't ring a bell or mean a thing to me, either. What does the other note say?"

Marcia opened it, and then leaned against the wooden counter for support. Her head buzzed, her stomach lurched. She was going to be sick.

Jared wrapped his arms around her and whisked her across the tropically decorated lobby to an easy chair under the palm trees that took up most of the open area. A small glistening pool gurgled over strategically placed rocks, replicating a waterfall lined with a profusion of red and yellow blooms.

"What does the second note say?"

"It's from my sister. Heather was rushed to the hospital for another blood transfusion. Her blood count dropped to almost nothing."

Jared scanned the hotel lobby.

"Jared…"

"Come on. Let's go."

"What? Do you think they're here watching us?"

Marcia checked the area. Nothing. No one appeared suspicious. But then again, she wasn't sure what she was searching for. She inched closer to Jared. He placed his arm around her waist and led her toward the entrance. His steps were steady, but hurried. She kept up. Tilting her head, she gave him a questioning look.

"Smile. Make it look as if nothing is wrong."

"I'm not some timid, clinging wimp."

A man sauntered out from around the middle of the foyer adorned in a profusion of varying shades of green tropical plants, and headed toward them. Dressed in casual slacks, a golf-type gray colored shirt, he held a cell phone in his hand, studying it as he walked across the room.

"Smile, dammit. Follow my lead."

Marcia's smile stiffened. She'd spoken too soon. She was a wimp. Her heart raced, and she was sure it was a combination of Jared's arms around her and the possibility that the man glued to his phone was headed their way.

Instead of leaving the hotel, Jared angled them toward the bar and an empty table next to the window. Marcia slid into the booth, and looked out the window in time to see the man looking back at them. He smiled, and never skipped a beat as he walked on by.

"Oh, my, God. He looked right at us." Marcia's hands flew to her chest, her eyes wide.

Jared had seen him, as well.

"He knows we're here. Should we leave?"

"Let's wait a few minutes. Do you want a drink?"

"No. I want to leave. That man gave me the creeps."

"At least we know what he looks like. He isn't one of the men who grabbed you earlier, is he?"

"No. Those men were stocky, muscular." Marcia shuddered recalling the incident at Christ the Redeemer.

Was this man a threat or a friendly local who happened to glance toward her as he meandered by? He hadn't looked threatening.

What had Russell gotten himself into? And how

the hell had she gotten involved?

Jared ordered two glasses of wine. When they arrived, Marcia gulped half the liquid in her glass despite the antibiotic she'd been given at the hospital. She only hoped it would calm her insides. She took a deep breath and took another swallow for good measure.

****

"I hope you had a nice rest and your side does not pain any longer," Sophia said later that afternoon. "Jared says you did not need stitches after all. *Excelente.* Still, it is wise you went to hospital to confirm you are okay. Let's go to the patio now and have a *café* before we leave for dinner. The men, they have stepped out for some *negócios*—business?

Sophia placed cups on the tray, poured the strong aromatic Columbian brew and headed out to the patio. Marcia followed the aroma outdoors. She welcomed the warm late afternoon heat and the shade of the trees and shrubs surrounding them. She sank into one of the cushioned chaise seats and put her feet up. The relaxing ambiance soothed her frayed nerves.

Sophia served the coffee, sipped from her own cup, and then placed it in the saucer.

"What do these *banditos* want from you?" Sophia sat down, sipped from her cup again and rested it in her lap. "Jared and Kurt, they think I do not need to know everything. They try to protect me. But I am concerned. How can I help if I do not know what is happening?"

"They think I have a flash drive with copies of Jared's avatar games—a prototype they assume my brother Russell is trying to sell to the Japanese."

"*Mon Duo!* I cannot imagine your brother would

do such a thing."

"Do you know my brother?"

"Oh, yes. He has been here with Jared, and sometimes stops by to visit while in Rio on *negó*…business. Such a nice man, your brother."

"Yes, I think someone in Jared's company is trying to frame him. Jared doesn't think so. I get the impression he thinks I'm working with Russell."

"*What*. I have not known you long, but I know you are not a bad person. And why would they be after you and your brother if you were working for such men? Jared—sometimes he can be so thickheaded. Like his brother, all they think of is work. Business. Bah. You must change his mind. It is time Jared find a lady to love."

Marcia gulped. The coffee, strong and hot, slid down her throat with a bubble of air. She swallowed. Took a deep breath.

"You have the wrong impression, Sophia. I'm not Jared's lady." She didn't know how else to make it any clearer without sounding uncharitable toward this very gracious hostess. Jared had had the opportunity two years ago and screwed it up. Marcia placed her cup back in the saucer.

"Ah, I see. You blush. He is a good man, our Jared. Works too hard, yes? No time for a love life for so long. It is time he let go. Give in to his feelings for you."

Seeing Jared again after all this time, and on the heels of her break up with Bradley was nothing but sheer coincidence. Having some of those feelings from two years ago resurface was baffling.

"The only relationship Jared wants is with his business and the Double R."

"This nasty business with Jared's company is a set-back. You will see. Jared will put it right. I see how he looks at you. Protects you. He will make time for you. I see it in his eyes."

Marcia wasn't so sure. Jared would always find something involving his work to occupy his time. He would never be able to consider a permanent relationship to interfere in his company and ranch. She wasn't going to wait around until he uncomplicated his life in order to make room for another person—her. She longed for a long-term committed relationship, and vowed to hold out for as long as it took to find one. Which, if she was honest with herself, might be never.

"Tell me, Sophia, how did you meet Kurt?" She hoped Sophia understood she didn't want to continue to discuss her relationship with Jared.

"Oh, my. He was just like your Jared. No time for me. He had to build the business—nose to grindstone, as you say. Once I met him, I could tell he was the one. On a silly prank, he and his friends joined my class to learn the *samba de gafieira* during *Carnaval*. Not the competition dance, but the ballroom dance—it combines some of the tango steps—very seductive. You will see. I will teach you. You will love it. I will take you to my dance hall to see my young students perform. These poor children, they need an outlet to get rid of their energy instead of running in the streets—doing drugs and causing a ruckus. And the costumes they wear—oh, so brilliant and sparkly. Wait until you see them in action."

"I'd love to see your students in action. Will they be performing for *Carnaval*?"

"Not at the big stadium. We are too small. We hold

our own competition with other neighborhoods in local halls. But as the dancers get older, they will strut their stuff, as you say, and hopefully be winners in the bigger competition during *Carnaval*." Sophia's giggle was contagious. "We will go tomorrow, yes. I will teach you so you can dance with Jared. We will go to the *Plataforma* and see a show, then to a dance club where you can do the *samba de gafieira*, too. It will be delicious fun. You will see."

"What kind of delicious fun are you cooking up now, Sophie?" Kurt stepped out onto the patio, leaned over, and gave his wife a kiss on her cheek.

Jared stepped onto the stone floor as well, hands in his pockets, looking handsome and pleased. Marcia's heart hitched a beat. Her talk with Sophia about Jared, sexy dances, and the possibility of being held in Jared's arms in one of those dances had her hormones kicking up a dance all their own. She couldn't take her eyes off him.

"We are going dancing, my love. Marcia is to learn the dance of Brazil."

"Talk of dance can wait until tomorrow. If we don't get going soon, we will miss our dinner reservations tonight." Kurt put his arm around Sophia, urging her along.

"I hope you have saved your appetite, Marcia. The food at Porcao's is fantastic."

Chapter Eight

Jared didn't know what Marcia and Sophia had been talking about over coffee, but the look on Marcia's face mesmerized him—a rosy flush, sparkling eyes, and a mouth slightly open and looking very kissable. If Kurt and Sophia hadn't been in the room he would have scooped Marcia up and kissed her senseless. After his meeting with his Rio office staff manager this afternoon, he was relieved to determine there was no way Marcia could be involved in trying to ruin his company. He had to admit, though, she might be right—her brother might be an innocent bystander. But who would want to frame Russell? He needed proof before he would concede.

When Marcia came down the stairs later that evening, ready to leave with the others, he met her in the foyer. She peered over his shoulder, raised her brows, and chewed her lower lip.

"Where did Kurt and Sophia run off to?"

Was she afraid to be alone with him? Had those come-hither eyes of earlier been deceiving?

"They went on ahead to confirm our reservations. Sophie didn't want you to feel rushed after your ordeal today. If you'd rather not go out for dinner, I'll give them a call on their cell."

The sly matchmakers purposely left them behind so Marcia would have to ride with him.

"No, no. I'm okay. In fact, with the light bandage on my ribs, I hardly feel any pain. And I am looking forward to this special restaurant. Sophia promised me it is an extravagant buffet with cuts of meat on skewers, sliced, and served at the table with such flourish. I would be impressed. I'm not so sure I can eat all that much to make it worth it, but I'm intrigued. And I don't want to let her down."

"I'm sure she would understand. Look..." Jared returned to the issue of her early morning attack. "I'm sorry about the assault at Christ the Redeemer. I shouldn't have let go of you—should have been more alert after your room was broken into."

"It wasn't your fault. Neither of us had any idea I would be followed. I don't know what they want from me—I don't have anything. And I don't have any information to give them."

"I've talked to Kurt. He's going to do some snooping into my computer files—see if he can break any odd-looking codes that might give us an idea of who's breaking into the files. He's a whiz at the keyboard. I've given him access. It's only a matter of time before we find out who is hacking into the files and stealing the prototypes before they are finalized and hit the market."

"Do you think these men are going to keep following me? I can't live with someone dogging my every movement. If it wasn't for needing to find out what happened to Russell, I'd be on the next plane back to New York."

He didn't want her to leave Rio without him. Not sure when these feelings had surfaced, he only knew he had to make every moment with her count. See where it was going. After…well…he wasn't sure what he would do once this was over, and they left Brazil.

"What's on Sophia's schedule tomorrow? I have another appointment with my associates in the morning, but I thought we could do some sightseeing."

"Sophia mentioned dance lessons in the afternoon, than the dinner show at the *Plataforma*."

"Right. She's quite the organizer."

"I'm looking forward to it—can't wait to see her in motion."

"She is a dance force to be reckoned with—be prepared."

****

Marcia squirmed in her seat while she took in the floor show—men and women scantily dressed, gyrating to the syncopated tempo, making love in front of the mesmerized crowd. An inner heat suffused her entire body. She couldn't take her eyes off the dancers, didn't dare look at anyone, especially Jared—not wanting to give away her own wild emotions that simmered below the surface. Were others in the dance hall as affected by this sensual, sexual performance?

The dance drew to a close, the audience clapped, whistled, and cheered as the dancers lined up on stage for their final bow. The dance floor opened for anyone wishing to join the performers. Jared extended his hand across the table and clasped her fingers, urging her to join him. She tugged against his hold, but he insisted. She caved and followed him to the middle of the crowd. Once he positioned their hold, as Sophia had instructed earlier in the day, he started maneuvering her around the room.

Jared's left foot slid next to her right foot, a

whispered caress, and then he tapped her foot quickly, suggestively. Marcia swung her foot to the right, stepped back with her left foot only to have his right foot follow suit. She held her breath. His leg nestled snuggly between hers, his one hand softly, firmly, clasped her hip. The other hand squeezed hers in a mind-blowing, tantalizing touch of seduction. She broke out in a cold sweat, trying not to look up into his dark eyes, afraid of what he would see in hers. But her eyes had a will of their own and refused to heed her warning. He focused on her face, simply waiting until she found the courage deep inside to return his look. She shivered when she saw the sensual, raw sexual hunger, a need matching her own heightened awareness so unmistakable, she gulped. Dance instructions with Sophia hadn't prepared her for the emotions overwhelming her now—being touched so seductively by Jared had her insides melting.

If her sister could see her now—standing in the arms of this tall, dark, handsome, sexy man, gliding around the floor in such abandoned ecstasy. He might not be Brazilian, but he simply oozed charm and danced like one. Her heart tripped over her feet, her body flamed, her mouth dry, she continued to let him make love to her on the dance floor in front of everyone as if they were the only two in the room.

Never in her whole life, all twenty-eight years, had she ever experienced anything so strong. This all-consuming need to become a part of someone else to the point of wanting to flatten her entire body against his. He held her firmly in his control, their bodies mere inches apart as he led her expertly where he wanted her to go. They continued around the floor, past the other dancers. Oh, dear Lord—there were other dancers on the floor and she had been about to…well, she wasn't sure what she'd been about to do, but it wasn't anything she wanted to do in public. She was so turned on sexually by the spell of the music and dance—and Jared. She'd forgotten they were in a room with more than a dozen other couples. Did Sophia's samba affect them the same way? The way it was totally seducing her? Did Jared feel the same sexual attraction?

The seductive steps continued—feet playing with each other in a dance that was nothing more than mind-blowing foreplay. Marcia swallowed again, her mouth as dry as cotton balls, her face hot, her inner core aching with the desire to fill the emptiness she realized had been there for some time. A need that a simple dance with a handsome man was able to fill? A very handsome, sexy man who was able to ignite the flames burning inside her, and was confident enough to do it.

The fast movements were such a rush—literally. It had her heart racing to keep time. It seemed as if the dance would never end, when suddenly the music stopped. Couples smiled at each other, hugged, clapped, laughed. Marcia, however, was spent. Unable to utter a single word, she found herself stepping forward, at the same time Jared stepped back. His hand still on her hip, he swung her around, gently, and with his other hand holding hers, led her off the dance floor without so much as a word. He released her hand when they reached their table.

Thankfully, she slid into her chair at the same time a waitress wearing a very skimpy brash glittery sequined outfit placed a tall icy drink in front of her. Marcia didn't hesitate. The frosted drink was cold to the touch as her fingers wrapped around the glass. The sweet, wet, soothing beverage slid down her parched throat. She drained half the content before lowering it and setting it back on the table. She didn't know what was in her glass, but it was cold, decadently sweet, and went down smooth and soothing.

Jared kept his eyes on her—the deep emotion emanating from his half-closed cobalt eyes confirmed he was as affected by the dance as she. They were attracted to each other. But did he have real, meaningful feelings toward her? Did it matter? She wanted him, she was ashamed to admit. Ashamed, and a bit guilty for having such feelings for Jared so soon after calling off her wedding with Brad. But heck, what did she have to lose? She needed...no...wanted to discover whether she was flawed sexually in some way. Find out if she had what it took to satisfy a man. So why not find out with Jared? After all, she was on her honeymoon—sort of. Why not embrace what he seemed so willing to give, wanted—a night of unbridled sex? Hmmm. Un-bride—that was her. A non-bride.

What the hell!

Jared couldn't take his eyes off of Marcia sitting across the table from him if he wanted. He all but drooled at the come-hither gleam in her sexy eyes. Damned if she didn't want him. And good God, he ached for her. They had played footsies on the dance floor for the last ten minutes as the seductive music belted out a beat. It echoed throughout every fiber in his overheated body. He'd worked hard to tamp down the sexual need surging through him when their eyes had met and held. It didn't work. *Damn.* If they hadn't been in a room full of people, he would have had her clothes off already. He would have had her sexy, naked body up close and very personal in seconds. And he bet his last dollar she would have been right there with him—all the way.

As it was, his body still ached for the hot, delectable body sitting across the table looking good enough to eat.

He picked up his iced drink and downed it in one gulp. But the cold fruity liquid didn't do a damn thing to dispel his need for this delectable woman. Watching her watching him hit him like a ton of bricks. He was about to cross a line he'd vowed never to cross while in Rio again. Her dazzling blue eyes spoke his name. *Caution be dammed.*

"Are you ready to leave this place?" Jared broke the spell she held over him.

At first she assumed he had had enough of her company and wanted nothing more than to get her home and out of his sight—take her back to the house. But when he latched onto her arm and all but dragged her across the crowded floor, then whisked her out the door into the cool evening, he maneuvered her back up against the building and kissed her. Hungrily. Sensually. She had no trouble figuring out what he had in mind.

And she was more than ready.

"My car is around the corner. Let's go."

She was glad it wasn't a question—she wasn't sure she would have agreed so quickly. But not given the chance made it easier to cave in to her sensitized hormones. She followed his lead, almost jogging to keep up with his long strides.

Jared tucked her into the front seat of his black

rental, and then ran around the front of the car to get in behind the wheel as if he was already late for an appointment. He had the key in the ignition, and drove away from the curb into the evening traffic so fast her head spun.

She held on to the armrest. Oh, Lord. Were they moving too fast? Were things out of control? Did she want to slow down? She looked out the window along the beach front. Several volleyball games were winding down. Lovers walked hand in hand, enthralled with each other, mindless of the surf lapping the shore. Birds skittered carefully around the water as it kissed the sand and slid back out to sea. Several vendors attempted to sell their wares to the tourists along the zebra-striped, wavy-tiled sidewalks.

Confused, Marcia's doubts wavered as they left the main beach area and expensive hotels behind. Jared drove away from the bustling traffic and sparkling nightlights. True, his kiss had tingled clear down to her toes. Toes being made erotic love to on the dance floor by his erotic toes.

Her face flushed hot. If anyone was to take her temperature at this moment, they would be stunned at how high and how fast the mercury shot up. She closed her eyes and took a deep breath. Oh, yeah, Jared had totally turned her on.

Jared made a left turn, inched the car into a parking area next to a small secluded beach, and shut the motor off. He slid his arm over the seat, behind her shoulders. His fingers played with wisps of her hair that had come loose. He wrapped a strand behind her ears, his fingers lightly sliding across her earlobe.

Was he about to make love to her here in the car? It

didn't matter. She was ready and willing.

He took her hand, raised it to his lips, kissed it, and then clung to it as if she'd disappear. Her heart fluttered and her insides squirmed. Was she honestly ready for this? *Oh, yes.*

"Changed your mind?"

Had he read her mind? She'd brooded over it several times since they'd left the club. She should say yes, she had changed her mind and ask him to take her home. The words stuck in her throat. She unbuckled her seat belt. But instead of taking her in his arms, he was out of the car and around to her side in a heartbeat.

The minute she stepped onto the sand, he drew her into a slow, warm embrace. Her arms circled his neck, and she clung like a needy child.

"Let's walk along the beach. We need to talk." He squeezed her hand as if she'd already agreed, and started walking, his hand gripped warmly in hers.

He was probably doing the right thing slowing things down, thinking things through. Leaping into a relationship was a terrible idea. Having feelings for Jared on the heels of an almost marriage didn't say much in her defense, either. Sure, she hadn't gotten over Brad's unfaithfulness, but she wasn't as broken up over losing him as she should be.

The moonlight was like a beacon high in the night sky. Stars sparkled brightly overhead, and the waves washed the shore. They removed their shoes, and strolled hand in hand in mutual silence for a few minutes. Several birds cawed overhead, and then dipped into the ocean searching for an evening meal.

"Jared…"

"Marcia…"

Still under his spell, her gaze locked on his. Despite the physical gravitational pull his nearness held over her, she stepped away as if it would clear her mind. It didn't.

"I think we need to slow things down until we find out what's going on between us, don't you?" Jared broke the spell.

"No."

He smiled, wrapped his arms around her and kissed her, leaving nothing to the imagination. One hand snuck between them and started unbuttoning the tiny delicate buttons on her silk blouse. It hadn't helped that the fabric had played a big part in the erotic emotions she'd experienced as the material had swept against her sensitized skin when they had danced, and now as he slid it from her shoulders. It whispered to the sand, tantamount to a sleek caress. Her skin squirmed in anticipation. Her body hummed at his touch, the cool breeze caressing every fiber of her being.

Bradley's arms had never, ever, excited her to this degree, had never made her tingle from head to toe. Had they danced? Never with such all-consuming sexuality and abandonment. He had never unbuttoned her clothing slowly, methodically, and with a look of pure sexual lust in his eyes. And he had never, ever, *ever,* made her feel all tingly inside like Jared did—with a single look, a mere touch.

Jared couldn't think beyond the reality that Marcia was actually in his arms, willingly. He wasn't sure how far things were going to go, but he damn well was interested in finding out.

He leaned in and buried his face in the sensitive nook of her neck and trailed kisses down over her shoulder and beyond. She tilted her head sideways, giving him better access. He took full advantage. He continued to sample what she so sweetly offered. He was totally lost when she sighed.

He lifted her into his anxious arms, pivoted, and made a mad dash for the crop of palms to their right. Thank God above she didn't resist. The sensation of her arms wrapped around his neck and her delectable body nestled into him… His heart was about to explode.

He laid her on a bed of grass and then knelt beside her. If body language had any merit, then there was no question she was more than ready. *Yes!*

He wanted to make absolutely positive she would be with him every step of the way.

"You're sure?" He raised his brows, his lips firm.

Her "yes" was barely a whisper, but he heard it. He smiled, then squeezed her hands and lay down beside her. Her lips on his were gentle. It was enough to spark and ignite his desires. There was no holding back. He took her lips in a demanding quest. Her ardent response was like a lit match to dry tinder—spontaneous combustion.

****

The overpowering smell of gas clawed at his nose. Cramped quarters, darkness, and the droning of tires hitting the pavement led Russell to conclude he was in the trunk of a vehicle. Having been out cold for heaven only knew how long, it was hard to tell if it was day or night. His head throbbed.

Hands tied behind his back, mouth gagged, Russell kicked at the hood of the trunk. A shooting pain circled his ankles. They were attached together. Several deep breaths and prayers later, he forced himself to relax. He prayed for a heaven-sent miracle.

Stay focused. You're alive. It's a start.

He sank back onto the stiff cramped floor. He'd had no idea selling secret prototypes to the Japanese was so dangerous. Who would hate him so much they would implicate him in their scheme? Who at Reed Technologies wanted to hurt him and his family? God almighty! Bea and Heather. He wished he could talk to them. See them. Tell them how much they meant to him. How much he loved them. Make sure they were safe.

The car slowed, and then stopped. Russell's heart beat erratically. He closed his eyes tight and prayed for strength to face whatever happened once the hatch was opened. Could he survive another beating?

Car doors slammed shut. Multiple feet crunched along the pavement. Definitely not sand. He understood and spoke Portuguese, but these men were talking too low and too fast. Their voices faded away from the vehicle, along with their footsteps.

Russell strained his hearing only to listen to their voices and footsteps grow louder as they approached the vehicle again. The only other noise he could decipher was the ocean as it slapped against something more solid then the beach. Boulders?

Where had they taken him?

The trunk swung wide and fresh sea air filled the cavity. It was dark, the men mere images, shadows.

"So, you have one more chance before we dispose of you. Tell us where the prototype is. Who is this Mr. Rose?"

A long thick arm extended into the trunk and ripped the duct tape from his mouth. He gulped and held back the scream, even though he was sure a good amount of skin had been ripped from his face along with the adhesive. Tears sprang unbidden. He swallowed twice. Did they see him wince in the dark?

"Now, you tell us what we want to know."

From the sound of their voices, they were the same men who had chained him to the bed and beaten him senseless. Simultaneously, one man grabbed his feet, while the other his hands. They lifted him with ease, swung him up out of the trunk, and dropped him on the ground like a sack of oats. His head hit a crushed stone pavement—stones jabbed into arms that were tied behind his back. He rolled to a stop against a boulder and closed his eyes. It was getting harder and harder to hold in such pain.

"This is your last chance, as I said. Reveal this Mr. Rose. Tell us where we can find the prototype?"

"I told you, I don't know. I don't know a Mr. Rose."

"Is it your sister? Marcia Kline? Is that why she was at your hotel—to get the prototype and dupe Mr. Osaka? To sell to highest bidder? Perhaps she is playing Mr. Reed against Mr. Rose to make more money?"

"*NO!* She is not involved. I'm telling you—leave her out of this."

"Last opportunity to come clean…"

"I told you the truth, I…"

"We do not need you no more."

Thinking the large man was after a gun, Russell rolled to the side, as far as his restrained body and energy would allow. A loud zap rang in his ears, and an electrical shock not only stung, but jerked him around like a firecracker bounding around on the ground trying to go off. Another zap followed the first one. He lost control, hit his head on something sharp—solid. And blessedly blacked out.

Chapter Nine

She had to be dreaming. Lying in the arms of one handsome, sexy man who had made mad, passionate love to her under a moonlit night in a secluded lagoon certainly was what happily-ever-after fairy tales were made of. It didn't happen in real life. Certainly not in hers.

Loath to open her eyes and discover it was only a dream, Marcia hung on to the sated warmth. It flowed through every vein, every pore, every portion of her sensitized body. Snuggled securely against Jared's taut skin, he held her as if she was the most precious thing in the world. She sighed.

"Are you okay?" Jared whispered.

He kissed her forehead as if in a tender tribute to what they had shared. She sighed again.

"Never better. I want to stay like this forever."

He shifted his hold. Oh, God. Was he letting her go? Did he regret making love to her already?

Oh, no. She should have held her tongue. Not implied she wanted forever. He wasn't after a forever kind of relationship. Darn. Darn. Darn. What was it about her that turned men away?

A muted buzzing pierced her thoughts. Jared shifted away from her, sat, and reached for his pants. The buzzing continued. She curled into a ball of rejected frustration. What would it take to become invisible? Pretend she hadn't just had the most mind-blowing sex in all of her entire life. She held her breath, swallowed the ache. Had their lovemaking meant nothing more to him than sex?

"Hello," Jared said, then remained silent as he listened to whoever was on the other end of his cell phone.

Oh, Lord. He had only released his hold on her to answer his phone. She composed her rampant emotions, wiped at her wet cheeks, and stared up at the bright stars overhead. He swung around, stared at her, eyes half-closed, not saying a word while he listened to whoever was on the other end of his cell phone. The minute he hung up, he inched close. She couldn't make out his facial expression in the shadowed moonlight, but she knew he was about to tell her something monumental.

"What's wrong?" Marcia managed, unable to stand the suspense any longer.

"That was Kurt. He had a call from one of his contacts in the *barrio*. They found an American man lying on the rocks on the other side of the bay."

"Oh, my, God. Is it Russell? Is he alive?"

Tears gathered. Her hands flew to her chest. *Damn! Where were her clothes?*

Marcia sat up and frantically searched for her clothes in the surrounding darkness. Finally, she spotted something resembling a white lacey scrape in the sand. She reached for it. Yes! Her undies. She gathered them, along with her bra, slacks, and blouse and with shaking hands put them on.

Shoes? Where the hell were her shoes? Oh, dear God don't let it be Russell. Let him be okay.

"Don't panic. We don't know if it is Russell. It's *Carnaval*, remember, there are hundreds of Americans celebrating in the streets. It could be anyone."

"But it could be Russell. You know it could be him."

He tugged her into his arms. She let him. He put his hand on her shoulder, lifted her chin with his other hand, and looked down into her watery eyes.

"They've taken him to the Copa D'or hospital. It's in the Copacabana area. Kurt says it's one of the best, which means he's being well looked after and is in good hands."

Jared wrapped his hands around her trembling fingers. It should have been comforting, especially after what they had shared, but it wasn't.

"Come on. Let's finish dressing, and I'll take you to the hospital. I'm sure the police will be there and maybe we can get a few answers. At least find out if it is Russell."

Jared finished buttoning his shirt and tucked it into his khakis. He bent down, retrieved something from the beach, and then handed her the shoes she couldn't find. They were full of sand.

"Did they have a description of the man?" She shook the damp grains out of her shoes and stepped into them, ignoring the grittiness.

"Kurt didn't say anything other than it was a tall American. Does Russell have any distinguishing marks to help identify him?"

He slipped his hand in hers, and they headed down the beach toward the car.

"A slight scar on his left shoulder from surgery. He dislocated his shoulder when he played football back in high school. I haven't seen it in years, so I'm not even sure it's visible."

"If he dislocated his shoulder and had surgery, the doctors most likely put a pin in his shoulder to hold it in place. It will show up in an x-ray. We'll mention it when we get to the hospital."

They reached the car, slid into the front seat, and fastened their seatbelts. Marcia's mind reeled as Jared peeled out of the cove and headed down the highway. Jared dropped her off at the hospital emergency entrance, and then parked the car. The waiting room was filled with a multitude of patients needing attention, including some very scantily clad late night, early morning revelers. Marcia remained waiting in line to find out if the man they had found on the rocky quay was her brother when Jared joined her.

"It's a madhouse in here." He shook his head. "Why don't you have a seat, and I'll see what I can find out."

"I'm fine. Besides, look around, there's no place to sit. I'll stand over by the window."

A tall, thin Brazilian couple, arms wrapped around each other, were making out in the far corner. A young mother with a baby and young child who couldn't stop coughing huddled in a single chair next to the door. An elderly man, bent over, wheezing, sat in a wheelchair, with a conservatively dressed, pretty young woman standing next to him patting his shoulder, a worried frown on her face. Marcia wondered how long they'd all been waiting to be seen.

There were two more people standing in line, one holding his hand in the air as blood dripped down his arm, the other shifting from one foot to the other. A sudden commotion to their left had everyone gaping to see what the fuss was all about. Two policemen entered escorting a young man in handcuffs, his head beaten and bloodied. They bypassed the line and escaped through a double swinging door.

Jared shot out of line, hot on their heels.

"Where are you going?" Marcia called after him.

"Stay put. I'll be right back."

Marcia followed without hesitation.

"I thought I told you…"

"It could be my brother in there."

The nurses' station resembled a zoo with everyone running around trying to keep up with the activity, reports, tests, results, and keeping everyone going in the right direction without let up. The strong smell of antiseptic solutions stung her nose. But there were other odors too—apparently from those who had emptied their stomachs after a night or two of celebrating *Carnaval*.

"We're here to identify a man—he arrived by ambulance an hour ago. Can you tell me what cubicle he's in?"

"There's been several ambulances come in. Let me check for you. Do you have a name?"

"Russell Kline. He's an American."

The nurse left the station and disappeared through a side door into an inner office while Marcia and Jared waited, trying to stay out of the way. A policeman appeared at their side.

"If you will come this way, please, we can talk." He held his hand out to the side directing them to a room down the hall. "We have two bodies, no identification. We believe one is American. And we have one we assume is American who is severely beaten, or taken a rather ugly fall off a rocky ledge. He is going to live, but he is currently sedated. They are running the usual tests to make sure there is no brain injury. However, I do not like to ask this, but we have no identification on any of these men. Before I have you go through claiming a body, perhaps you can give me some specific features your brother might have, in order to make this process easier on you."

The question was intended for her, but it was Jared who answered.

"Her brother has a scar on his left shoulder from an earlier surgery. Do any of these men have a scar?"

The officer flipped through his note pad, then shook his head.

"I do not see mention of this. However, the doctors are working on the one. I will check. If you will have a seat, I will be back shortly."

Marcia paced the floor.

What if Russell was dead? How could she break the news to Bea? Such news would be difficult for them to cope with, on top of Heather's being in the hospital.

Jared could only imagine what was going through Marcia's mind as she wrung her hands and paced the small private waiting room. If Russell was one of the men in the other room, he hoped like hell he was the one alive. Not only did he want it for Marcia's sake, but for Russell's family's sake, as well. And to be honest, he figured Russell had the missing piece to the puzzle. If it was Russell selling his prototype, he didn't know how he was going to deal with his betrayal. Especially, after spending such a mind-blowing night in the arms of the most incredible woman with whom he'd ever made love.

God help him, he had to agree with her. He'd wanted to stay right there with her wrapped in his arms forever—naked. It had been so damn good. So right. Never better. He was sure they would have continued to make love over and over again until the break of dawn if it hadn't been for his damn phone ringing. He'd wanted to toss it in the water and let it wash out to sea. Despite the current situation, he'd wanted nothing more than to feel her naked body up against his again. He shook his head as if it could dispel the urges still raging inside. He had to stay focused. He had to help her get through this ordeal. If it wasn't Russell who lay in one of those cubicles, they needed to work harder to find him before something did happen to him. And he'd be there—right by her side.

"Miss Kline." The policeman entered the room.

Jared shot to his feet. Marcia's hands swung to her chest, the look on her face broke his heart. She expected the worst. He put his arm around her shaking body and held tight. She leaned into him. He strengthened his hold, and waited for the officer to break the news one way or the other.

"It seems the deceased man is not your brother. They are checking for the scar on the other American. They will let us know as soon as they have an opportunity to do so. In the meantime, I will need you to answer a few questions, please."

Jared led her over to the sofa and settled in next to her.

"We only know her brother—Russell Kline—has been missing for several days. His hotel room was broken into, as was Miss Kline's. We assume whoever broke in was searching for a flash drive that came from my company. We reported it to the police when it happened."

"Yes, and no one seemed to be concerned." Marcia stepped forward, her hands fisted at her side. "Maybe if they had been, Russell wouldn't have ended up beaten and left for dead."

"We don't know if it is your brother." Jared reached over and took her hands in his and squeezed them. She was wound too tight. It wouldn't help their cause if they upset the current officer. He relaxed when he felt her tension subside.

"We will confirm soon," the officer reiterated. "As I say, the doctors are checking for this scar. What else can you tell me about this break in?"

Finally, an official interested in the situation.

Jared filled the officer in on the details leading up to tonight.

"We returned to the hotel to ask if Miss Kline had any messages. There was one—it insisted she hand over a flash drive if she wanted to see her brother alive."

"And did she give them the item as requested?"

"I don't have one to give to them or anyone else. How could I return it?"

The man eyed Marcia as if she had two heads. About to explain, he was interrupted when a young man with a stethoscope around his neck walked into the room. He nodded to the policeman, spoke in Portuguese, then left. From what little Portuguese Jared could decipher, Russell's condition was critical. The policeman's translation confirmed it.

"The x-rays prove the man in the other room is your brother. They have placed him in I.C.U. He is unconscious, but alive. The doctor says he has a broken leg and wrist, which they are currently setting. If you would like to get a coffee while you wait, please to ask one of the nurses at the station. They will help you. If you will excuse me, I have other matters to attend. I will be in touch if there are further developments. I'd appreciate you contacting me directly if you learn of anything that will help us apprehend whoever did this."

"Thank you." Jared shook the officer's hand. "We will be sure to keep you informed."

While Marcia used the facilities to freshen up, Jared made his way to the nurses' station, and was directed to a tiny kitchenette where a fresh pot of coffee sat on a neat counter with various creams and sugars. He poured the steaming brews into two Styrofoam cups, helped himself to two wrapped pastries sitting in a basket next to the assortment of bagels, and then made his way back to the waiting area. He handed Marcia her cup and pastry, took a hearty sip from his own cup, and then escaped to go find the facilities. He splashed cool water over his face, straightened his shirt. He had no doubt Marcia wasn't involved with whoever her brother was involved with. If she had any idea who was behind this, he was confident she would have come forward to the police at this point. Wouldn't she?

When he entered the waiting area, Marcia sat in an uncomfortable-looking sofa, her head tilted against the back, her eyes closed. God, she was beautiful. His heart lurched at the possibilities. The what if's. The what could be's. God help him if she was involved in this scheme.

She finished the pastry and set her empty coffee cup on the end table. Already it was 4:00 a.m. and neither of them had had any sleep. Hell, he was wide awake, which was good because they had a long wait ahead. He finished his now cold coffee and downed the tasteless apple-something pastry he couldn't even put a name to. Hopefully, the strong Columbian coffee would kick in and keep them going.

Jared took his cell from his belt clip, walked out of the room, down the hall, and outside the hospital into the cool morning air—his finger on Hank's speed dial number when he hit the door. He didn't give a damn what time it was back in Oregon. He wanted answers, to find out if the P.I. Hank had hired had checked out the benefit Marcia mentioned. Why would she lie about a thing like that? Russell was a religious man and attended church with his family on a regular basis. But he had heard no mention of a benefit. He would have been more than willing to donate to the cause.

He checked his watch while he listened to the phone ring in his ear. It was five hours' difference, which meant it was 11:00 p.m. in Oregon. Hank could be anywhere—he wasn't one to head to bed early unless he was with a woman. Too bad if that's where he was. He wanted answers. *Now.*

Jared paced under the hospital emergency room portico, the silence in the morning air annoying.

"Come on. Pick up," he muttered. He swiped his hand through his already tousled hair. About to leave a message on the answering machine, he heard the click of it being connected on the other end.

"What's up in Rio, buddy," Hank slurred.

Which meant he was probably at the local dance hall if the noise in the background was any indication.

"Russell was badly beaten and left for dead. He's

in the hospital and unresponsive. Have you dug up any information on the contacts he was supposed to meet down here?"

"Damn. He must really be involved with some pretty dreadful dudes down there. Is he going to live?"

Jared wasn't sure. He hoped so. For his wife's sake. For Marcia's sake.

"I'm here with his sister. He's in I.C.U., so we haven't been allowed in to see him. Apparently, he has a broken leg and wrist and a severe cut on his head. Probably a concussion. We don't have all the reports on his tests."

"His sister? The hot one? Wasn't she about to get married?"

Yes, the "hot one"—Hank had no idea how hot.

"She mentioned something that wasn't in your report. I want you to look into it ASAP. Check out a benefit Russell's church apparently held for the family. According to Marcia, there was a huge donation which covered all of their expenses and then some. Find out what you can and let me know. It might explain the instant income on his bank statements."

"I don't understand why they didn't contact us for a donation. Not sure how the P.I. missed it. Will give him a call and put him on it first thing in the morning. Have you met with any of Russell's regular contacts to see what they know?"

"Not yet. I have an appointment with them later this afternoon. I need those other names and addresses."

He'd been so caught up with Marcia since he arrived in Rio, he'd almost forgot about meeting with his reps. One of the reasons he didn't do relationships well. He needed to stay focused on business. Find out who was selling him out. Still, it was hard to put what they'd shared a few hours ago out of his mind.

"Get me those contacts. Fax them to my brother. We're staying with him."

"We? Weren't Marcia and her new husband staying in one of those swanky hotels along the beach?"

He didn't want to get into the reasoning behind Marcia staying at his brother's, or why her "new husband" was absent. Matter of fact, he'd like to know the real reason she was here on her own, too.

"Look, Hank. Get me this information as soon as you can. Check out the new techs we hired, and the new hand we hired for the ranch. Make sure they're legit. I need to get back inside. I want to be there when Russell wakes up, and find out what happened. What he knows. I'll talk to you later."

****

Oh, God. She'd been making love with Jared while Russell had been beaten within an inch of his life and left for dead. It was a miracle he hadn't been washed out to sea. The thought of her being in the arms of the man who was accusing her brother of selling him out, sickened her. How could she let herself be taken in by the sensual rhythm of the Brazilian ambiance—they had practically preformed foreplay on the dance floor, for heaven's sake. The sultry evening breeze washing over her sexually charged body on a secluded beach with a very virile, handsome man she was half in love with already had blown her mind. Not to mention she needed, wanted, to be loved after being dumped by her fiancé. Find out if there was something sexually wrong with her.

God, what a disaster. She was a failure. Jared's

hesitation, in spite of whether or not his phone had interrupted them, only proved what they had shared hadn't meant the same to him as it had to her. Obviously, he still wasn't ready for a serious commitment. Not to mention she'd let it slip her mind that he was trying to prove Russell was the one out to ruin his company. How pathetic was that?

"Marcia?"

Marcia opened her eyes to find Jared standing over her. She hadn't heard him come back in and didn't know how long he'd been standing there. She rubbed her eyes and sat up.

"Have you found out anything?"

"No. I was talking to Hank back in Oregon. He's going to fax more information and put our P.I. on the case to see what else he can find. If Russell isn't the one selling me out, then someone else is. They'll keep digging until they find whoever it is."

"Jared…about earlier tonight. I think we got caught up in the whole *Carnaval* atmosphere—the music…the dance…I hope you didn't take it the wrong way thinking it meant more than it did."

"Don't do this to yourself. You're under a lot of stress right now. We both are."

"You're right, of course. It's not about me. It's about Russell…and your business."

"I'm not sure where you think you're going with your train of thought, but you have to admit the two are intertwined. And it is about you. Don't forget, your room was ransacked too. You've been threatened along with Russell. We disregarded those facts when we made love."

"Jared…"

"Let's take it one day at a time, Marcia."

"Excuse me, Miss Kline. Mr. Kline has been moved to a private room. Please to follow me."

Marcia rose, walked past Jared, and followed the nurse down the hall. The I.C.U. was busy, the telemetry monitors moderately noisy. An I.V. drip hung next to Russell's bed, and a blood pressure cuff was strapped to his upper left arm. Russell lay drugged, immobile, and nonresponsive. His wrist and leg were wrapped in a plaster splint, giving it time for the swelling to go down before setting it.

"There is nothing we can do at the moment. Why don't we go home and get some rest. We can come back later."

"Not an option. I'm family. I want to be here when he wakes up. Let him know he's not alone, that someone cares."

"At least come sit in the waiting room where it's more comfortable and quiet. I'll have one of the nurses come get you when he wakes up."

Marcia slid the vinyl cushioned chair closer to Russell's bed and sat. She wasn't leaving Russell's side until he woke up so she could talk to him. Make sure he was okay.

****

Water splashed over his cold body. Weak, unable to move a single achy muscle, Russell lay sprawled face down in a shore lined with jagged boulders. His head pounded in rhythm with the heavy surf as the water continued to beat his already battered body. Another wave washed up against the rocks covering him. He held his breath waiting for the tide to recede. A large piece of driftwood slammed against his shoulder. His legs flapped haphazardly, partially twisting him sideways. Tied. His legs were tied tight. Dear Lord, he had no control of his hands. He held his breath as another stronger wave slapped over him in a crushing blow. He was smacked against another jagged rock before being lifted on the water, then thrown back down as the tide flowed back into the ocean. In a panic, he jerked his body upright and managed to get a foothold between two smaller boulders, and wedged himself tight. He willed his body to cooperate with his mind, and remain in a standing position while the waves continued to ebb and flow around him, beating against his tired, aching body. Russell's exhausted countenance gave out. His chest hurt with each breath, the last breath more of a gasp as he was overcome with fatigue. Another wave knocked him over, his body contorted as he made one last effort to break free.

"Russell? Russell. It's Marcia. You're safe now. Relax."

Someone was shaking his shoulder

" Russell? Can you hear me?"

He took deep breaths, opened his eyes, and tried to sit up. He couldn't. He had to be hallucinating. What was Marcia doing in Rio? Right. She was on her honeymoon. He looked around the room. Where was he?

He blinked and attempted to focus. I.V. tubes hung next to the bed. He was alive. In hospital. He closed his eyes, sighed, and relaxed as best he could. He'd been through hell, but was safe. But for how long?

"Russell? Russell. Can you hear me?"

"Sis? What are you doing here? Where's Brad?"

"Don't worry about me. Relax. How are you

feeling?"

"Dead. They've filled me full of pain meds. Thank God. You have no idea the pain I've gone through."

He couldn't move his leg. He looked down and found a white cast securely affixed from above his knee down to his ankle. No wonder he couldn't move his leg.

Great. Bea was going to freak out when she saw him.

The blood pressure cuff kicked in and tightened around his upper arm. A nurse entered and approached his side. He spotted Jared in the doorway. What was he doing here? In Rio?

The nurse quietly checked his I.V., took his other vitals, nodded to Jared and Marcia, then left.

"Reed," Russell acknowledged his boss, his voice weak and shaky. "You didn't come all this way in a rush to visit me in hospital. How long have I been here?"

"No. I've been here a few days looking for you. What happened? Who did this?"

Russell wasn't sure he had all the answers Jared was after. After what he'd been through since coming to Rio, it was time to fill his boss in on what he'd found out.

"Someone is trying to sabotage your company. They're framing me. As long as I was in Rio on business, I wanted to help figure out who was selling your latest avatar DVD. Guess it backfired on me."

"Other than getting the hell beat out of you, did you learn anything?"

Russell didn't like the sneer on Jared's lips as he stepped closer to the bed, a sure sign he'd already nailed him as the guilty party.

"I'm being framed. They think I'm a Mr. Rose. Or the Rose."

"Is that your cover?"

"I don't have a cover. But it seems to be a good one. No one knows the Rose's real identity. They beat me twice trying to get the information out of me. Insisted Mr. Rose worked for your company. I didn't have a name to give them, so they beat me again."

Russell closed his eyes, sank back into the pillows, and sighed.

"Do you have anyone in your employ with the last name Rose?" Marcia raised her brows and bit her lower lip.

Russell opened his eyes, again, waiting for Jared's answer.

Jared stared at Marcia as if he'd suddenly realized she was there. Russell frowned. What were the two of them doing here together?

"Not that I'm aware of. But I've got Hank checking it out. We have a P.I. on the trail."

Russell didn't want Jared to know about Marcia being implicated as the Rose. No need to alarm either of them—she had nothing to do with it. Then he remembered that the thugs who had beaten him had said something about searching her room.

"You haven't had anyone accost you, have you, Sis? They told me they searched your room."

She looked first at Jared, then back at him before she answered. Something was going on between the two of them, but his light-headed brain wasn't able to figure it out. His eyes drifted closed, his breathing slowed.

"No. I'm fine. I'm staying with Jared's brother

Kurt and his wife, Sophia."

"Great…where's   Brad…is…is   he…staying …there…" His voice sounded hollow to his own ears, as if he was drifting through a hollow tunnel. His eyes shut. He blinked, tried to focus, but it took too much effort. He relaxed against the pillow and let the meds take hold.

"His pain meds have kicked in." Jared put his arm around her shoulders. "He needs to rest. We should get going, get some rest, too. Get something to eat. We can come back later when he'll be more alert."

"I need to call his wife. Let her know what's going on."

"Do you think it wise with their daughter in the hospital, as well?"

"I'll call my sister. She'll know how to handle Bea. It's the type of news you want to impart in person, not over the phone."

Chapter Ten

"We'll be at Kurt's soon. Rest your head and relax."

"How can I relax? My brother has been beaten and left for dead and is lying in a hospital bed on the brink of death. And someone wants me dead as well."

"You don't know that they want you dead. Let's think this through. Wait until we get to Kurt's—you can get something to eat and lay down for a bit. We can discuss this later—when we're not falling asleep on our feet."

Jared put the car in gear, backed out of the hospital parking space, and headed down the main highway.

"You've got to understand the kind of man Russell is." Marcia laid her head back on the headrest. "If he's being accused of wrongdoing, or if someone is being wronged, he'll go out of his way to prove their innocence. To get proof. If he needs to save somebody's butt, or the company in this instance—yours—he'll put his own life on the line. It's the kind of guy he is."

"You make him out to be a martyr. No one asked him to put his life on the line for me or my company."

"No. He's a man with very high standards and is thankful for those who stand by him and his family. Like you, he's looking for proof, only in his case, to prove he's not guilty. Don't you think he needs to prove his innocence to his family?"

"If he thought there was a problem, he should have come to me immediately. We could have nipped this in the bud. Listen, if you insist we talk, then tell me honestly—why are you here in Rio? Why now, when Russell is here on assignment? Is it really a simple case of coincidence?"

"What are you accusing me of? Why not come right out with it? Judge me along with Russell without proof of our innocence. You think I'm the Rose?"

She glared, stunned, and so disappointed at how quickly he could change from a sexy, satisfying lover into a man who didn't trust her. A man who assumed she was in cahoots in destroying Reed Technologies.

She was a fool once again.

"Marcie…"

"Don't call me Marcie. You don't know me well enough."

"You think not? After last night?"

"Last night was a mistake of the biggest proportion. Next to finding my fiancé in the arms of my aerobics instructor being right up there. But coming to Rio on my own to show that jerk I can get along without him and his ilk seems to take the cake. Seems I've gone from one more disaster into another. And I'm not talking about the men chasing after me for something I don't have."

"Dammit."

"My thoughts, exactly. Now, if you don't mind, you can drop me off at any hotel along the way. I'll find a room somewhere."

"Not likely. You aren't safe on your own." Jared turned the car into the Barra district. "You stay by my side until we figure out who's after you and who did this to Russell. As soon as we get back to my brother's, you can take a shower, relax, and get some sleep. You'll feel better."

She didn't think she would ever feel better again. Tears sprang to her eyes, threatening to escape. She looked out the window not wanting him to see how badly her heart was broken. What did he know about being cheated on by the man you expected to marry? About being made such sweet passionate love to only to be let down like a load of crap? Did the man not have feelings? If he did, was he so able to turn them on and off like a spigot when he so chose?

Her chest heavy, she closed her eyes and leaned her forehead against the side window. The car's air conditioning did nothing to cool her inner turmoil. All she ever wanted was to be happy. Find someone to love, settle down, raise a family. Was that really too much to ask?

Apparently, it was.

Jared drove into the drive and cut the engine. Marcia shot from the car and was taken aback when Sophia greeted her at the front door and enveloped her in outstretched arms. Unable to control the tears any longer, she broke down with much embarrassment, and sobbed all over Sophia's slim shoulders.

"Oh, my dear. I'm so sorry for your brother. Such a sad situation. The hospital is a good one. They will make sure he will survive this horrid ordeal."

Thankfully, Sophia misunderstood her tears thinking they were for her brother.

"They are doing all they can at the moment. Marcia needs rest. If you will get her a coffee, I'll take her to her room. She's exhausted."

"Of course. You will take care of her. I will get the coffee and some pastry Kurt bought at the bakery this morning."

Marcia drew back and took a deep breath, holding herself together. She didn't need Jared taking her anywhere.

"I can make it on my own, thanks. Coffee does sound lovely, Sophia. I'd love a cup," she hiccupped.

"Nonetheless, I will make sure you make it up the stairs in one piece."

Jared put his arms around her waist. She stepped out of his grasp, and tripped up the first step. He didn't say a word, but once again captured her and pulled her close. Despite her chaotic feelings at the moment, she was tempted to rest her head on his shoulder. Breathe in his scent. Nuzzle her face into his neck. Feel the caress of his skin against hers one more time.

God, she was pathetic?

"Jared."

"Later." He opened the door. "Take a shower. Sophie will have refreshments for you when you're done. Get some sleep. I'll be right next door if you need me. We'll talk later."

She turned, ready to refuse to be told what to do, only to see him close the door behind him on his way out. He left her standing, torn between being glad he hadn't pressed her further, and wanting him to take her in his arms and tell her everything would be okay.

Yep. She was totally pathetic.

The bed looked inviting. If she caved in to her desire to sink onto the bed and into oblivion now, she'd never make it to the shower. Although a soothing bath sounded much better, she was too tired to immerse her exhausted body into a fragrant tub of water for fear she'd fall asleep and sink.

True to Sophia's word, a tray with steaming coffee and pastries waited on the stand next to the bed when she finished her shower. A note with her name on it sat on the tray. Thinking it was from Jared, she took her time and devoured the scrumptious fruit pastry and downed the strong coffee. She gave into temptation, fluffed the pillows against the headboard, and sank into the deep cushioned mattress, and only then opened the letter. Her eyes popped wide in astonishment at the words childishly scribbled in awkward strokes. She closed her eyes, dropped the note in her lap, and took a deep breath. How to sneak out of the house tonight, and make her way to Sugar Loaf Mountain to meet with the men who had information about Russell's abductors? Without Jared catching her in the act? Instructions were clear—she was to come alone or they would find a way to kill Russell and his family. They knew he was in the hospital. It wouldn't be hard to end his life. But what about Bea and Heather? She couldn't let anything happen to them. She had to go. But to go alone? She clutched the note, shut her eyes and prayed for the courage to do this one thing for her family.

Where had the note come from? Who sent it? Sophia must be aware of it—she'd placed it on the tray. Was she aware of its contents? The sender?

What a mess. She had the whole afternoon to figure out how she was going to leave without Jared knowing what she was doing—where she was going. She didn't want him following her and risk putting her family in danger.

****

"What the hell is going on, Jared?" Kurt cornered him the minute he stepped out onto the patio.

"I wish I knew." He swiped his hands over his face and sat down in the padded wicker chair next to the railing. "I talked to Hank. He didn't have any new information. In fact, our P.I. didn't know about the church benefit and the major donation given to the family. The more I think this through, the more I'm beginning to believe Marcia. I don't think Russell is the one selling my company out from under me. I've got Hank contacting our P.I. to dig deeper."

"I know Hank has been your friend since grade school. You don't think he's the one trying to ruin you. Do you?"

"What? Hell, no. He's been with me through thick and thin. Even offered to work for nothing in the early years to help me get the business off the ground. His wife almost divorced him before she died because he spent so much time at the office. Why would he do that, then try to ruin me?"

"Money."

"You forget—he has money. They inherited a bundle from his wife's grandparents a couple years ago. His in-laws were loaded. Then there was his wife's life insurance policy. No. Hank doesn't need my money."

"Can you think of anyone else who has it out for you? Hire any new employees lately who might have a questionable background?"

"I've racked my brain trying to come up with someone. Anyone. Can't think of a single soul. Cash hired a new hand, but he came highly recommended."

"What about another company? A competitor who

has hacked into your computers to steal your material?"

"Hadn't considered that. I called Hank from the hospital. He's going to check with our P.I. tomorrow, his time, to see what else he has uncovered. In the meantime, I have a meeting with my Brazilian and Argentinean office in about an hour. If Russell's met with them recently, they might know something about other possible contacts he might have down here."

"Do you think the culprit could be someone in Rio?"

"Why not? It won't hurt to check them out. Know a good local P.I. I can hire? See what they can come up with?"

"Marcelo Costas. Although I haven't used him before, he is a friend. I'll ring him while you're at the meeting."

"Thanks."

But two hours later, after meeting with Russell's usual contacts, Jared didn't have any answers. He stopped at the hospital to check in on Russell, but Russell was still under the influence of medication and was nonresponsive.

****

"Where do you think you're sneaking off to?" Jared boomed.

Marcia jumped back, hitting her elbow on the door frame. From the tone of his voice, she could tell she had some explaining to do.

"I'm going out."

"Out where?"

"Just out."

"Not at this time of night and not alone. It's *Carnaval*. Too many crazies out there. Wherever it is you're going, I'm going with you."

"I don't need a shadow."

"Really? How many times have I saved your ass since you arrived in Rio?"

He had a point. It might be wise to have someone with her. She really didn't want him to know where she was headed. And why. But she didn't have time to waste, and she really, really didn't want to go alone.

"If you must know, I'm meeting someone on top of Sugar Loaf Mountain."

"Who do you know in Rio who wants to meet you there at this time of night? What do they want?"

He was much too nosey by half.

"Come on, Marcia. You don't look happy about this meeting. What's going on?"

"I received a note asking me to come to Sugar Loaf at eight o'clock. They want me to bring the flash drive. They said if I give them the prototype, they'd give me information about Russell's attackers."

"And you believed them? That does it. I'm going with you. No arguments."

"You weren't invited. I need to go alone."

"You aren't going anywhere until we talk this through. What are they going to do when you don't give them what they want?"

She didn't have an answer. She hadn't thought that far ahead.

"Damn it. To hell with this damn game. It's caused too much trouble already. Come with me. I'll have Kurt download something on a flash drive in his office. At least you'll have something to hand over to these assholes. And for the record, I am going with you—it's not an option open for discussion."

Marcia heaved a heavy sigh. Whether it was in frustration or relief that she didn't have to do this on her own, she wasn't sure.

Another tropical day in paradise—yeah, right. If it weren't for trying to find out who had beaten Russell to within an inch of his life and left him for dead, she might have been able to enjoy the ride up the mountain. Something she had been looking forward to doing before all hell has broken loose and Russell had been beaten.

Kurt sat behind his computer when they knocked on his study.

"What's up?" His smile quickly twisted into a frown. "Shit. What's going on?"

"Marcia got an invite to hand over the prototype at the top of Sugar Loaf. We need something authentic looking to hand over. Think if I give you access you can download one of my prototypes from my files to a flash drive? Like, in the next ten minutes?"

"Hey, is the Pope Catholic? Give me your password, and I'll do it in five. Have a seat."

Jared stood behind his brother where the two of them worked their magic. Marcia sank into an easy chair next to the window. She clasped her hands in her lap to hide her shaking hands. Even her legs shook. This was more involved than she'd anticipated. What were these men going to do when Jared showed up? Would they take the flash drive, accept it? Or question its authenticity?

"Done. What do you think this will get you?" Kurt handed Jared the mock-up.

"Time. And maybe another lead we can follow. It won't hurt. And damn it, I honestly don't care about this game any longer—it's caused nothing but pain. It almost caused Russell his life."

Without a word, Jared motioned for her to follow him out the door and into the car. They left Kurt standing, shaking his head.

Chapter Eleven

The lift up to the first hump on the way to the top of Sugar Loaf was done in silence. They were the only two waiting for a ride when the car glided around the rails into position. They stood on the painted footprints on the pavement next to the lift, ready to step inside. Jared helped her into the empty bubble-type contraption. Before they had a chance to grab onto one of the poles in the middle of the car, the machine kicked in and with a jerk, they were lifted off the platform. It swung out and over the forest far below—they were on their way to the top. Marcia adjusted her feet to coincide with the smooth sway of the lift, and let out the deep breath she'd been holding.

Would the men approach her with Jared by her side? Or would they leave and not share information which might help them find who had beaten Russell?

Silently, she focused on the view—the bay, the ocean, the tropical forest, and the clear, but darkening blue sky. It didn't help. Her insides trembled.

The lift shook violently, and then stopped with such force the contraption swung back and forth like a pendulum. Oh, my, God! If it broke off, they would end up careening far below to their death. She clung to the pole, digging her feet into the floor tiles. She couldn't get a secure grip.

Jared drew her tight against his taut body, and

together they sank to the floor. She flung her arms around his back. He immediately maneuvered her around to the front of his body and held her tight. She clung to him as if her life depended on it. *Oh, God!* Her life did depend on it. Nausea engulfed her insides. He wrapped his right arm around the center pole, and dug in with his rubber soled sandals. Hers weren't as serviceable. Finally able to form words, she voiced her worst nightmare in the middle of his chest.

"What are we going to do? How are we going to get down out of here?"

"I'm sure it's nothing more than a minor malfunction. They'll have it fixed in no time. We'll be on our way before you know it."

The cable car steadied. They untangled their bodies and slid to the floor. Marcia clung to the metal pole, not daring to let go in case the car started rocking again. Jared stood, looked around, and then quickly squatted down next to her again.

"How you doing down there?" He didn't meet her eyes. "You doing okay?"

"What do you think? How long are we going to be stuck up in the ozone in this death trap?"

He looked out the window toward the top of the mountain and the station overhang.

"Are you ready to make our escape?" he asked, his voice even, commanding.

"Are you crazy?" Her eyes popped open, her eyebrows rose in surprise. "In case you aren't aware of it, there is nowhere to go. Didn't you say they'd have this fixed in no time?"

His stiff body and guarded look frightened her. His eyes were trained on the overhang on the top of the mountain. Marcia turned to see what had Jared acting so peculiar, and froze. Two men were standing at the controls. One had a pair of wire cutters in his hands trying to snip the cables.

"Oh. My. God. We're going to die, aren't we?"

"Eventually, but not today. Have you ever rappelled down the side of a mountain? On a drag line?"

"No. Oh, no. What are you thinking?"

"I'm thinking it's the only way we're going to get out of this alive."

"You have got to be kidding."

"No joke, I'm afraid."

"Stand still. You're making the car rock again."

"Sit in the middle while I find us a way out of this contraption. As soon as I get my hands on something to wrap around the cable, we'll rappel down to the lower station."

"I'm feeling light headed. I don't think I can do this."

"Sure you can. I've done it a million times. Piece of cake."

"Easy for you to say. I'm sure I don't have the strength in my hands or wrists to hang on to anything long enough to let me slide down those cables. I certainly am not going to go down it like a monkey with my hands and feet wrapped around it."

"Hey. You were a cheerleader, if I recall. Don't tell me you never did pyramids. And didn't you mention something about working out at a gym? You can do this. All you have to do is hang on to me. Just don't let go. Ready?"

She blinked back tears. Tears weren't going to save

them. She took a deep breath.

"Yes. I'm ready."

"Trust me?"

"Do I have a choice?"

"It will go a hell of a lot better if you trust me."

To her surprise, she did. Regardless of their past and their botched relationship, she did trust him to rescue her. If she had to decide between Jared and Brad to save the day, she'd pick Jared any day.

"I do trust you. Tell me what you want me to do." She gulped and stood straight as if to prove she had everything under control.

"First, forget about those two men. They aren't there. Do not look at them. Do not look down. I want you to go to the other side of the car, slowly, so you don't rock the car. Then turn your back toward me, kneel down and cover your head. I'm going to kick out the glass up above and I don't want you to get cut with flying glass. Then, we're going to climb out on top, and you're going to wrap your body around mine and clasp your wrists tight. Wrap your legs around my waist and hang on for dear life. Pretend we're hang gliding. I'll do the rest."

"I told you, I've never hang glided before."

"Piece of cake."

"Yeah, right." She slowly made her way to the opposite side of the listing car.

The visions she had of her body wrapped around his in such a tight embrace took her mind off of the two men trying to cut the cables and send them to their deaths. A loud crash and the splintering of glass as it landed and splattered on the floor had her stomach lurching. She turned to find Jared shaking shards of glass off his clothes. She shivered.

Just another day in paradise! Right.

"Ready?"

"As I'm ever going to be."

Jared hefted his body up through the broken pane, and then extended his hand down for her to grab.

"Give me your hands."

Oh, God. This was it. It was really happening. She sent up a robust prayer and grabbed his hand. He clamped his around her wrists instead.

"Wrap your hand around my wrist and hang on tight. Ready?"

He didn't give her a chance to respond. He lifted her out into the openness and plunked her down on top of the car. The car rocked. Her head spun, her limbs wobbled. He put her head down between her knees.

"Deep breaths. You're doing fine. We're going to get through this. But we have got to act fast. Stand up slowly and hang on to the cords attached to the main cable behind you."

Without question, she did as instructed.

"Don't look down. Look at me, and only me."

She did. She saw the concern in his eyes as well as his determination. She trusted him. But then he reached down and unbuckled his belt, and in one smooth swish, pulled it out from around his waist.

"Jared…"

"Don't panic. It's our way down."

"How is you taking your pants off going to save us way up here?"

"My pants aren't going anywhere just yet. I thought you trusted me."

"I do." She was beginning to wonder if she did.

"Good. Now, I'm going to turn around and squat down a bit. As gently as possible I want you to hop up onto my back, wrap your arms around my neck, and grab hold of your wrists, not your hands. It will be a firmer hold. At the same time, wrap your legs around my waist and lock your ankles together in front of me. Do you think you can do that?"

She nodded. He shifted his body, never leaving contact with hers. He squatted, his one hand braced against his bent knees, the other never letting go of the cable. He caught her butt in a firm hold with his very masculine, strong hand and hefted her into a snug position. Before she had time to change her mind, he let go, grasped his leather belt, and slung it over the cable so that the large silver buckle was on top. He latched the belt together and grasped the strap in a tight white-knuckled grip. Without hesitation, he leaned forward, and they were gliding into thin air.

Marcia swallowed her fear. Her heart pounded so loud she was sure it vibrated right through her clothes against Jared's back. She rested her head against his neck and made an effort to think herself into a better place. Visions of being snuggled in Jared arms, on a secluded tropical beach came to mind. Her legs tightened around his middle, her breasts nestled more snugly against his back. Sensations rocketed through her lower body—an erotic emotion that had her mouth going dry, her mind buzzing with sexual desires.

"Honey, this isn't the time to get all caught up in a sexual fantasy back there. You keep squirming against me and we'll never get to enjoy the dream you're dreaming. There is no way I can accommodate you at the moment—as much as I'd really like to. You're making it awful difficult for me to concentrate on getting us down to the bottom—safe, and in one piece."

The belt jerked on the cable and caught. They were stuck in mid-air. Marcia held her breath, tightened her hold. Jared gripped the belt, yanked it up over the bulge. The motion sent the belt buckle slipping over the hump in the cable and had them surging forward—they were on their way once again.

Taking a deep breath, Marcia clutched closer. They were going to make it.

The cable slackened. They only had several yards left to go. Would the men slice through the cable before they reached safety?

Despite Jared's warning about holding on too tight, she couldn't help herself—she wished herself part of him. As one, they continued their journey downward. Jared's legs swiveled out in front of his body. His muscles tensed in her grip as they neared the landing. Yes! They were going to make it.

The cable loosened again. Jared changed tactics at the last minute. He threw his legs back and his body forward, let go of the belt, and dove toward the platform before they made contact. She caught her breath and held it as their bodies hit the pavement. As one, they landed, and then rolled head over heels, over and over, never-ending. Jared gained control only to collide against the inside station wall with a thunk. Their arms and legs twisted and tangled awkwardly. Momentarily stunned, she thanked her lucky stars they'd made it down before those two jokers up above had a chance to cut the wire all the way through.

Jared disentangled himself carefully, making sure not to cause her any further damage. She ached from top to bottom, and prayed she hadn't suffered any broken bones.

"Are you okay? Anything broken? What about your ribs? You're not bleeding anywhere, are you?"

"No. No blood. Nothing broken. Just my pride. I can't believe I did that—and am still alive to question my sanity. And yours."

He glanced over her shoulder. "We have an audience."

A crowd had gathered and were gawking at them— men with lecherous grins on their faces, women is concerned scowls. One young man had a video rolling, obviously thrilled he'd captured the entire descent. God, she hoped they weren't going to end up on the six o'clock news somewhere.

Jared stood, dusted his pants and shirt off, and then extended his hand to help her to her feet. She took it, only to be pulled into his arms. She clung to him. He kissed her—a quick kiss that left her more shaken then the ride down the wires. Camera be damned. She kissed him back.

"Can you stand on your own?" he asked, releasing his hold.

She took her time and rubbed her smarting butt.

"Landing mostly on my backside saved me, I'm sure. That, and the fact you cushioned my fall. If this is what it feels like to hang glide, I'm not interested."

"You did great—you're a natural. Give yourself time to get over this, and you'll be begging me to take you."

"Not in this lifetime. I've had enough of a rush today. I don't need to repeat the experience."

"Come on. Let's get going before those two goons

call in for back up."

Hand in hand, they elbowed their way through the crowd and down off the mountain to the car.

"I think we should check on Russell—make sure he's okay and someone hasn't gotten to him."

"You've got it, sweetheart. We'll report this incident to the police, as well."

****

Jared waited until after breakfast to call Hank to see if he'd uncovered more information. His friend picked up on the second ring.

"I talked to Russell's main contacts, and they don't seem to know anything about his schedule. They weren't supposed to meet with him until day after tomorrow, so they hadn't missed him."

"Did they have any information about the Rose? Any other contacts Russell might have down there?"

"No. That's the puzzling thing. They aren't aware we even have a problem. I checked on sales, as I'm sure your P.I. has, and all of them proved legit and on track. The only new item they were talking to Russell about was a new account with a Mr. Osaka. Seems he changed his mind at the last minute and withdrew his offer. Have your P.I. check him out. Did you find out anything else?"

"No. But we may have a problem." Hank's words changed from pleasant to snappish over the phone.

"What kind of problem?" God, they didn't need another crisis to contend with right now.

"There's another P.I. nosing around in our business. Did you call in someone else to investigate?"

"Hell, no. Why would I? Who is it?" He hadn't had a chance to make contact with Marcelo Costas yet.

144

"A company out of New York. Top notch, according to reports."

Jared heard papers being rustled around on Hank's desk.

"A company by the name of...wait...here it is...Holcomb & Holcomb Investigative Services. Listen, Jared, if you don't trust me and the P.I. I hired, just say so."

"Are you listening to me—I didn't hire anyone. Again...why would I? Is everything okay back there? Something happen I should know about?"

Jared couldn't help thinking about what Marcia had said about someone trying to frame Russell. Had Russell hired a separate P.I. to investigate his company before he left for Rio? "I want our own P.I. to dig deeper. I don't think Russell is the guilty party. I talked to him briefly—he's pretty sedated in I.C.U. But I'm sure he knows something he isn't telling me."

"Is he going to live? How bad was he beaten? I understand he was left for dead. Damn, man, that sucks. Is there anything I can do—contact the family? His church?"

"No. His sister has been in contact with his wife. Damn it, Hank, Russell doesn't need this on top of everything else. His daughter Heather is back in the hospital. His wife must be frantic with worry."

"All the more reason he needs to come up with more money—sell your prototypes."

"From what Marcia says, the church benefit raised a bundle, which got him out of debt. Have your P.I. check it out."

"Quite a bundle, even for a church benefit."

"I agree. But it was given by an anonymous donor.

See if your P.I. can get a name. See if it traces back to the business. Or the ranch. Someone is trying to do us in."

"I'm on it, Jared. What about this other P.I.?"

"Contact him. Better yet, have our P.I. contact him. Maybe they can work together and find out what the hell is going on."

"Good idea."

"You might want to cancel our rock climbing trip. I'm going to be tied up here for a while until this nightmare is cleared up."

"Be careful. If they find out you're digging into this down there, they might not have any problem beating you up like they did Russell."

"I'm more worried about Marcia. They seem to be targeting her now. They think she's the Rose."

"The Rose!" Hank laughed. "Is she as beautiful as a rose? Has she gotten inside your 'other' head now? You're not involved with her, are you?"

"As much as I might like to be, I'm not into long-term relationships. You know how I feel. I'm still trying to build the business. Need to figure out who wants to see me go under."

"But you've already succeeded in both Reed Technologies, as well as the Double R Ranch."

"One would think, seeing as someone is trying to ruin the business. Look, Hank, if you find out anything, let me know. Anything. No matter how insignificant it seems. It might be the missing link. We're missing a very important piece to this damn puzzle."

Jared signed off and clicked his cell shut. He sat for a few more minutes. Who was this other P.I.? Who hired him? What did he want? Was his client the Rose?

He was sure the piece to the puzzle was right in front of him. He hoped it didn't have anything to do with Marcia. No matter what he'd said to Hank, his feelings for her had him thinking a short term relationship wasn't going to be long enough. Especially, after they had made love.

The way he had wanted to make love to her two years ago.

She'd been soft in all the right places. His hands had finally discovered every inch of her smooth, delicate skin the other night. He hardened just thinking about her—how she fit in his arms as they'd danced so close—every inch of her touching every inch of him. And on the beach—she had shivered with anticipation, shimmied closer to him as they lay in the sun-drenched sand, the sensations of their love-making filling him until they exploded into a sweet, exhilarating climax together. Waves slipped over the sand in rhythm with his heartbeats—or was it Marcia's heartbeats? A dance as old as time—the tide stopped for no one. He had to agree with her—he'd really, at that moment, wanted nothing more than to stay right there in her arms forever. Being interrupted, however, had landed him back to reality in spades.

Why would Holcomb and Holcomb P.I. be investigating his company? Holcomb? Wait a minute. Was that Holcomb—as in Bradley Holcomb? *THE* Bradley Holcomb who was supposed to be married to Marcia?

Jared inserted the key in the ignition, revved the engine, and drove up the winding road to his brother's. He and Marcia were going to have a little chat. He wanted answers, and he was sure Marcia had some she'd been keeping secret.

****

"I visited Russell at the hospital last night," Marcia told Sammie when she called her after her morning coffee. "Tell Bea he's doing the best he can under the circumstances. A few broken ribs, his right kneecap is shattered, and he's had a severe blow to the head. They're keeping an eye on him, keeping him sedated. He's still in I.C.U."

"I'm sorry you have to bear the brunt of this on your own."

"Honestly, I wish I never left New York. But I'm glad I'm able to keep an eye on Russell and be by his side when he opens his eyes again. So how is Heather? Has she been discharged from the hospital yet?"

"Doing much better. They did another blood transfusion, changed her diet, and want to keep her stress-free. But they sent her home. Said she'd get more rest if she was in her own environment."

"I hope Bea isn't sharing information about Russell's situation with her?"

"Of course not. I haven't told Bea all the gory details. She's had enough to deal with."

"Is there anything else we can do for Heather?"

"No. She'll pull though this once again. And as long as they keep catching it in time, they'll be able to treat it. Think she might even outgrow it as she gets older."

"I hate to have you be the one to tell Bea about Russell. I know you'll break it to her gently—be with her for support. I know she appreciates all your help. God, Sammie, I can't believe Russell is guilty of anything other than trying to clear his name. These men are coldblooded—leaving Russell for dead. I don't think I'm the one who should be down here helping him. In fact, I've got to tell you, whoever these men are, they think I'm involved."

She wasn't about to tell her sister about the hair-raising experience she and Jared had survived on Sugar Loaf. She could hardly believe she'd done something so daring—even if it was to save her own life. Jared's ingenuity had saved them.

He was her hero. Well, hero worship wasn't all that had her throwing her body into his arms. The tension running through her on their wild ride down had her flying high on sexual emotions—she hadn't given their danger a second thought.

"What?" Sammie interrupted. "How do they figure you're trying to undermine Jared's company? You aren't even connected with it, or live in the same state."

"They think I have one of Jared's latest prototypes. They insist I'm holding it back from the Japanese for more money. Even Jared thought I was involved, working with Russell."

"How ridiculous."

She didn't mention the subterfuge in preparing a flash drive to give the men, which they never got. Would they come after her? After Russell?

"Did you arrange for Brad to check into Jared's company?" She hated to ask the question, but she really did want to know if Brad had refused to investigate because she'd walked out on him. And she wanted to divert Sammie's mind away from her own personal problems—that she and Jared had been thrown together in a very sensual/sexy part of the world. Especially, during *Carnaval*, where emotions ran high and libidos ran rampant. Never mind the danger they've been dealing with since she arrived.

"Yes. He was only too happy to help." Sammie sounded too gleeful. "I think he's sorry he cheated on you. Wants to make it up to you. Isn't charging us a dime."

"I don't want him back. Sammie, you should have made it perfectly clear. I don't care if he didn't want to take the money. We could have found someone else." Marcia's hand tightened on the receiver, her stomach churned. *Please, please, please don't let Bradley come to Rio*, she pleaded under her breath.

"What?" Sammie asked.

"Nothing. Did Brad find out anything?"

"Yes. The money donated to the church for Heather was withdrawn from Jared's business."

"What? You've got to be kidding."

"He followed the money," Sammie snickered. "Isn't that what P.I.'s always do—follow the money? The cashier's check was drawn on the same bank where Jared's accounts are held. Don't ask me how Brad got the information, but the same amount donated to the church was withdrawn from one of Jared's minor accounts."

Marcia sat down and leaned back in one of the twin wicker chairs situated either side of the stand where the phone sat. Did Jared know his money had been used to get his own employee out of debt?

Could life get any more complicated?

The front door slammed seconds before Jared appeared in the doorway. He glared at her as if she sported three heads with purple dots. Her first thought was that Russell had died. Then, as he approached, she drew back at the glaring steel in his eyes. Her heart raced, her mouth went dry and her hands shook.

"I have to go, Sammie. I'll talk to you later." She hung up before her sister could respond. Paralyzed by his stare, she waited.

The look in Jared's eyes, his stance, was controlled—menacing. After what they had been through—hero or no hero, she refused to be cowed. She stood so he couldn't look down his nose at her. She squared her shoulders and let him have the shocking news before he could say a single word.

"Are you aware the money donated to Russell's church came from your bank account?"

It stopped him in his tracks. His lowered brows and squinty eyes told her he doubted her facts.

"What are you implying?" Jared's voice was low, even, modulated.

"That a sizable anonymous donation given to the church specifically targeted to cover the loans Russell had taken out on the house was drawn on one of your bank accounts."

Jared looked over her shoulder, out of the window overlooking Sophia's tropical gardens. Marcia could see her words were sinking in. He held himself erect— he'd connected the dots. He swung his gaze back to her, an intent look on his face.

"I'm sorry. Apparently, my P.I. didn't have such information or he would have provided it. Which reminds me, you don't happen to know a Holcomb & Holcomb Private Investigative company based out of New York, do you? The name Holcomb ring a bell?"

So that explained why he'd been so upset with her when he walked in. Bradley had ruffled feathers back in

Oregon. It hadn't taken long for Jared to get the news in Rio.

"You know I do. And, yes, he is my ex-fiancé, and he's a P.I. My sister Samantha hired him against my wishes. However, it's a good thing she did, otherwise we wouldn't have found out about the money having been withdrawn from *your* account. How did that happen?"

He shook his head, and stared at the floor as if the answer lay at his feet.

"Have you had *your P.I.* check into my banking accounts, too? Do you still think I'm involved in selling your stupid avatar games out from under you?"

"No. I had no cause to think you were involved before I left for Rio."

"Which means, you have cause now? Oh, God. I really am stupid, aren't I? You've been coming on to me, seducing me, to get information. You don't care for me, do you? It was all a ploy to see what you could find out. The dance, the kiss, that fiasco on the secluded beach—it was all a game to you. Like two years ago."

Not waiting to hear what excuses he'd come up with, she walked out the side door toward the patio, around the corner, and headed to the gardens. Tears streamed unabated down her checks.

She circled the gardens, the house, and headed down the drive at a fast pace toward the beach. He didn't follow. If he'd had any feelings for her at all, he would have followed her out the door and called her back. If he'd had any feelings for her two years ago, he would have asked her to stay then. He hadn't, and there was nothing saying he would, now.

One more crappy day in paradise.

****

Jared speed-dialed Hank's number. How had their P.I. missed this? And more to the point, was Marcia correct? Did someone send the church a certified check from one of his accounts? And if they did, who the hell had done it without his authorization? *My God, someone was stealing him blind as well as selling his DVD's?* There were questions that needed answers. He'd have Kurt check into hiring Marcelo Costas to go over his books. And soon.

Hank's voice mail clicked on. *Dammit!* Where the hell was he?

"Hank. Jared here. Give me a call. There are a few details I've discovered which need to be checked out and addressed in regards to this whole mess. Have your P.I. dig deeper. Apparently, the New York P.I. found a check drawn on my account and sent to a church benefit for Russell and his family. Contact me as soon as you find out anything."

Jared snapped his cell shut and walked in the house in search of his brother. Damn it, he needed to talk to someone. He passed Sophia on the way to the patio.

"You go. Sit. I will get refreshment for you to cool off, as you say. Miss Marcia is out in the garden."

Jared found Kurt on the patio, his feet kicked up on the end of a foot stool, leaning back in his easy chair.

"So, trouble in paradise?"

"This is getting more complicated."

He sank into one of the cushioned chairs and rubbed the palm of his hands over his face.

"Love is like that."

"What the hell are you talking about?"

Kurt laughed outright. Jared shook his head.

"I'm talking about this whole mess with my company. I want to make contact with your P.I. Something isn't right. I need an impartial investigation. I'm beginning to believe Marcia. Someone in my own company wants to see me ruined, and they're framing Russell."

"From the conversation you had with her, I assumed her ex-fiancé was on the case. Don't you think he can be impartial?"

"I don't give a damn about him. I want someone we can trust down here. Find out if Holcomb is correct."

"If you really want one more P.I. involved, I'll give my guy a call. Put him right on it."

"Yes, but let's keep it under wraps. I don't want anyone back at the ranch to know about it. I'll give Costas access to everything—say the word. Tell him to keep it confidential."

"What about Hank?"

"What about Hank?" Jared trusted him with his life. There was no reason why his best friend would have cause to undermine his company. If the business bellied up, then Hank would be out of a job, too.

"If he found out, he might inadvertently let it slip to someone else. It could jeopardize the investigation."

Was Kurt right? He didn't want to mess things up. Jared thought about it for a minute. "Okay. Tell your guy to try and be as discreet as possible."

"That's what P.I.'s do. Now, are you going to sit and stew, or are you going to go after Marcia before one of those thugs gets a hold of her again and she ends up in a hospital bed next to her brother?"

"*Shit.* I was such an ass. I didn't even think she

might still be in danger."

"You might want to apologize when you find her."

"For what?"

"I couldn't help but overhear your conversation—it wasn't exactly a quiet one. Be thankful I was the one who overheard, not Sophie. She'd be on your case big time. Go. Apologize. I saw her go down the drive. Make sure she's safe."

Jared glared at his brother. Kurt raised his eyebrows. Jared collected his car keys and headed down toward the beach. Hopefully, Marcia hadn't gotten very far and she'd be easy to spot.

****

Once on the main street, Marcia kept heading toward the beach area, her mind blank. She didn't know what to think, didn't want to think. She simply walked at a quick, steady pace until she found herself across the main drag and in the middle of an almost deserted beach. Everyone except her was sane enough to stay off the beach during the hottest time of day—the beach broiled with the already spiking temperatures.

She was thirsty, but being in such a snit, she hadn't taken the time to grab her purse, which of course meant she didn't have any money to buy a cold drink. Disgusted with herself, and with Jared, she kicked at the sand and plunked down despite the heat. The coarse hot granules heated her bottom in seconds. She wished she had a towel or blanket to sit on. She lifted her pant legs, rested her elbows on bent knees, and laid her face in her hands.

And let the tears flow.

Exhausted from her walk, and drained from the late night, having zip-lined down from Sugar Loaf

Mountain, the worry over her brother, and her niece's health issues, she had no one to turn to—no shoulder to cry on. She refused to call Sammie again. She didn't give a damn about Bradley and her failed almost-marriage. She lifted her head and gazed out into the sparkling sea, the blinding sun. Sweat trickled down her forehead, her neck. She sure could use her hat and sunglasses she left sitting on the table in the entranceway. The water mesmerized, the shimmering waves gently slapped against the shore beckoned. How easy it would be to wade out and drift away.

A hand grabbed her from behind, restraining her. Strong, meaty hands snaked under her arms, lifted her shoulders. Before she could dig her heels in, she was dragged along the hot sand, unable to get a foot-hold. Good Lord, they were kidnapping her, and there was no one to stop them. Shoulders and elbows immobilized, Marcia forced her body to go limp. She needed to save her energy and wait for the right opportunity to take action. Whoever these two men were—probably the same two who had attempted to kill her the night before—they would have to let her go sooner or later. Whether it was to shove her into a vehicle, or stuff her into something, she'd be ready.

She had been hauled several yards when she was unexpectedly dumped on her butt so hard she was sure whiplash was about to set in when her head and back hit the beach—hard. Sparkling stars blurred her vision. Not sure what had just happened, she was nevertheless grateful to be free. A throbbing headache caused her stomach to churn. She flipped over, rose up onto her knees, and emptied her stomach before she had a chance to see who they were or where they went.

She flinched when a hand rested on her shoulder, and held her head down. Shit. They were back. Marcia groaned. No doubt about it, if given the opportunity, she was going to book the next flight home.

"Are you okay? How's the cut on your ribs? It's not bleeding again is it? Did they hurt you?"

She sat and gazed up at Jared. He held her hat in his hand. She tried to smile, but her lips trembled, and it didn't come off as convincing as she intended. She wiped her mouth with the back of her hand.

He had followed her after all.

He helped her to her feet.

"No, no bleeding. Not hurt. Just taken by surprise. Thanks for coming to my rescue."

"Here. You forgot your hat. The sun can be deadly this time of day."

"Yeah, so can the beach."

She took her hat from his out-stretched hand, and plunked it on her head. Taking a couple of deep breaths, she willed her stomach to behave and her legs to stop shaking.

Jared put his arm around her back and walked her to a group of palm trees.

"It's shadier under the branches. Have a seat."

She leaned against one of the tree trunks. He sat down beside her. His nearness had her inching closer. The heat intensified. She took a couple more steadying breaths to calm her chaotic emotions. Sun sparkled off the water. She'd put her sunglasses on, but she'd left them behind on the stand in the hallway, as well.

Jared reached in his pocket, removed her shades, and handed them to her.

"Mind telling me what the hell just happened?"

She took several more calming breaths, willing her body to stop shaking. She was still madder than a wet hen at him. But she longed to lay her head on his shoulder, feel his arms around her again. To have him comfort her.

Damn it, she wanted him.

He'd followed her. Saved her ass once again.

"I guess they're not giving up trying to get their hands on the prototype."

"What did they say?"

"They didn't say a word. Just took me by surprise, and started dragging me off the beach. Probably those two goons who trashed my hotel room, lured us to Sugar Loaf Mountain, and have been following us everywhere."

"Were you able to get a look at them?"

"No. They snuck up from behind. They strong-armed and dragged me off."

"You shouldn't have stormed off on your own after what you've already been through. It isn't safe. Think you have nine lives?" He brushed his hand over his windblown hair. "Haven't you learned your lesson after the episode on the mountain?"

"I'm not guilty of anything except coming down to Rio de Janeiro to get away from my pathetic life."

"You've got to admit your involvement looked suspicious when I first met you outside your brother's room. Both of you were in Rio at the same time, and both you and your brother's rooms were ransacked. And all the information I was given pointed directly to Russell. I'm sure these men are thinking along the same line."

"All circumstantial." She kept her eyes out to sea,

her voice low, unemotional.

He was silent for a moment.

"I agree. I told Hank he needs to dig deeper and see if he can find out who sent the money to the church. Do you know where your P.I. got his information?"

"No. I told you I wasn't the one to contact him— my sister did. But you have to admit it looks as if someone in your company, other than Russell, or at the ranch, wants to see you go under."

"It's a possibility I have to address. And I am. Trust me."

Trust him? She'd trusted him enough the other night when they'd been entangled in each other's arms, and look where that had landed her. More confused than ever. Especially, after he'd rescued her again.

"Are you okay? Ready to go back now?"

"Yes. I need something to drink. Something with plenty of ice."

He was considerate enough not to comment on the temper tantrum that had her landing in trouble once again.

Lesson finally learned.

Chapter Twelve

Jared made his way to the gardens as soon as they arrived at the house. Marcia had escaped to her room. He wanted to follow her, but he needed to walk off his pent up frustrations. Sophia's gardens were extensive. It was a good spot to unwind. And he was in bad need of unwinding.

Seeing two men dragging Marcia along the beach had had his heart palpitating triple time and his legs sprinting faster than a marathon runner's. Visions of her lying in a hospital bed, beaten and left for dead like her brother, had almost undone him. They'd spotted him bearing down on them, shouting like a crazy man, and thank God they had let her go before they took off. Dammit, he would have given chase, but they'd fled to their van and driven off before he had a chance. In any case, his concern had been for Marcia—to make sure she wasn't injured when they had dropped her like a sack of feed.

Hiding his feelings from her hadn't been easy. Watching her lose her stomach contents made him feel inept. He'd wanted to rant and rave and kick asses. Those men had a lot to answer for—if he ever got his hands on them…

It was hard to believe Marcia was in cahoots with whoever wanted his technology company to go under. If it wasn't Russell, it had to be someone else inside who worked for the company. Who the hell could it be?

He ran his hands through his hair, down over his face, and gritted his teeth. *Damn it to hell.* How many times was he going to have to rescue Marcia before her good luck charm wore off. Keeping her safe had become a full-time job. Granted, it was one he was more than happy to comply with. But what would happen when he wasn't around to help her. To keep her safe? What then?

They needed to seriously discuss the situation. He needed to make her take precautions until they found the culprits and locked them away. He needed to apologize to her—for a lot of things. Mainly, because he knew in his heart she wasn't guilty. And...well...just because.

****

A knock sounded on Marcia's bedroom door. She rose from the chair next to the window and crossed the room. She and Jared hadn't exactly parted amiably on the beach, and she wasn't ready to talk to him. Holding her breath, expecting him to be on the other side, she opened the door, and let out her breath.

"Marcia. A handsome American is waiting downstairs to talk to you." Sophia grinned.

"A visitor from America? Are you sure he doesn't want to speak with Jared? Did he say what he wanted?"

"No. Come. Find out. He waits on the patio. You will have privacy."

Why would someone be looking for her here in Rio? Could it be someone with information about Russell? About Jared's prototype? There was only one way to find out.

Marcia stepped out onto the patio, and froze.

"Bradley! What are you doing in Rio? At Kurt and Sophia's house? How did you find me?"

Bradley rushed to her side, arms open wide.

She ignored his gesture and sidestepped out of reach.

"Whoa. That's not a very warm welcome, Marcie. I thought you'd be happy to see me."

"You're kidding, right?"

"Well, technically it is our honeymoon. We could…"

"You have the nerve to mention *our* honeymoon? Get real. Honestly, Brad, why did you come all this way to Rio?" Never mind he'd had to purchase another ticket, seeing as she had his ticket in her purse and hadn't gotten around to tearing it up.

"Listen, Marcie. I made a mistake."

"I repeat, what are you doing here, Brad? And, how did you find me?"

"Easy. When I checked in at the hotel, they told me you had left. They informed me someone had broken into your room. That you were staying at Kurt Reed's place—they gave me this address. I assumed he's Jared Reed's brother. It wasn't hard to put two and two together. So here I am. Why aren't you staying at the hotel like we planned?"

"How could I stay there after someone rifled through my belongings?"

"They haven't rented it out yet? We can take advantage of it."

"Don't you get it? It's over."

"I'm sorry, Marcie. I don't know what came over me. What I was thinking. She came on to me—seduced me. Honest. If you'd given me half a chance to explain before you walked out on me…"

"I walked out on you with good reason. Don't tell me it was the first time you cheated on me. Your actions said otherwise. Your 'lover' implied otherwise."

"Damn it. I said I'm sorry. I traveled all the way to Rio to apologize."

He stepped closer, reached for her hands. She had all to do not to step away again. She had to prove to him once and for all that his nearness, his touch, his charismatic personality didn't have the same effect it once had. She was no longer emotionally involved with the man standing in front of her, who wrongly considered she was about to forgive him. It was a relief to finally admit she truly didn't care for Brad—didn't love him.

She had let go.

"It doesn't make any difference, Brad. I am not head over heels in love with you. I might have been upset when I left New York, but it didn't take me long to discover I wasn't as hurt as I should have been. In fact, you probably saved us both from a disastrous marriage."

"It's him, isn't it? That cowboy wannabe?"

"What are you talking about? What cowboy?"

"Jared Reed. His ranch, his business, his money. He's a millionaire two times over."

"He runs a ranch. What does that have to do with anything? He also owns a successful technology business, as you very well know."

Brad thought it was all about the money? She hadn't known Jared was such a wealthy rancher and businessman—didn't care. It was all moot, anyway. Jared had no interest in her, other than a means of finding out what Russell was up to.

"Leave Jared and his money out of this. He has nothing to do with what happened between you and me."

"Ah, Jared is it? Pretty cozy—living under the same roof."

He hauled her into his arms in a tight clinch, claiming her as his own. Before she could protest, he kissed her. Instead of protesting, she remained impassive. It was a kiss meant to make another man jealous. But it was a kiss that left her cold.

She heard the door slide open behind them. She struggled to inch her hands between them in an effort to push Brad away, but it was too late. Jared burst through the door, a scowl on his face—she wanted to run in the other direction.

****

He had to stop it now. It was out of control and the entire operation was about to go under. Why Jared had to play the macho employer and go to Rio in the first place was beyond him. If he'd stayed at his damn ranch, all of this would have worked out and no one would have been the wiser. And it didn't help that Russell's sister had to show up in Rio and gum things up further, or that Russell had written to Jared, implicating him. With Jared out of town, it was easy for him to intercept the letter. He'd had no choice but to put Osaka's henchmen on the job—to find out just what Russell knew, and what he was up to in Rio.

The plane landed in Sâo Paulo and taxied up to the terminal. Hank grabbed his carryon and stood in the middle of the aisle along with everyone else impatiently waiting to get off the plane. He wasn't used to flying commercial, but Jared had his company jet sitting at the airport in Rio. And he wasn't on company time or funds. This time, he planned to stay under the radar.

The call from Mr. Osaka hadn't been pleasant. Either he came to Rio with another copy of the prototype, or they had no deal. His threat to expose him for passing off illegal documents pissed him off. Shit, the Jap had to be calling his bluff. Who was he to turn him in—Osaka was practically stealing from *him*. The price he planned to pay him wasn't exceedingly lucrative. But it was sufficient to facilitate his goal of breaking away from Reed Technologies and starting his own business. He'd made enough contacts over the years—he wouldn't have to start from scratch.

Hank made his way through customs. He'd arranged to rent a vehicle before leaving Oregon— thankfully, it was ready. He keyed Mr. Osaka's address into the GPS system, calculated the time it would take to arrive, drove out of the parking lot, and headed northeast.

****

Jared's insides contracted. He stared through the patio's glass sliding doors. Marcia was in the arms of another man. Their embrace revealing. His heart thudded clear to his feet. He couldn't see Marcia's face, but it was obvious she welcomed the sexually intimate kiss from her ex-fiancé. Had her P.I. come to apologize, sweep her back off her feet, and march her down the aisle to the altar? His insides churned at the picture they presented. How could she be in the arms of another man after the night they had shared—making love on the beach? His gut wrenched. His jaw clenched. His fists knotted.

Damn it all to hell, he'd lost his chance—twice. He'd been a stubborn headstrong idiot two years ago, and now...hell. He'd almost lost his business and now he'd lost the woman he loved.

Loved! Yes, dammit. He hadn't been able to get her out of his mind since he'd met her two years ago. And now it was too late to do anything about it.

Jared closed his eyes, not giving a damn if he interrupted them or not. He drew his shoulders back, shoved the door to the side, and stepped out into the warm tropical heat. He tucked his hands in his pockets to steady them, and pasted a smile on his face. He forced his feet to make their way to the couple. They stepped apart when he approached. Jared gritted his teeth, and heaved a deep breath out from between tight lips.

"Sorry to interrupt, but Sophia said Mr. Holcomb was here," Jared addressed Marcia's fiancé. "I assume you have information pertaining to Russell Kline, Miss Kline's brother, to help exonerate him?"

Bradley Holcomb dropped Marcia's hands and stepped away—but not far. He offered his hand in greeting. Jared wanted to ignore the gesture, but thought better of it. He accepted it.

"Mr. Holcomb." He nodded.

"Please, it's Brad."

"*Mr. Holcomb*, I want to thank you for stepping in and helping with this case. I know you did it as a favor for Marcia and her family in order to clear her brother's name. I am grateful."

"My pleasure. It also gave me a chance to come to Rio—get out of the cold New York weather and to meet with Marcie so we can work things out."

Jared wanted to knock Bradley Holcomb's cocky grin off his clean-shaven face. The man wasn't good enough for Marcia. He might be a good P.I., but he was a rotten cheat. It probably wasn't the first time the man had cheated on Marcia, and it more than likely wasn't going to be the last. He looked at Marcia and wanted to warn her, wanted to take her in his arms and tell her he loved her. He wanted to kiss her, make love to her. But she stood staring at him as if he were a stranger. As if they had never been locked naked in each other's arms.

"Right. Well, then, I'll make sure you're fully compensated for your work…"

"No need. As you said, it was a favor for Marcie. I managed to talk to the hotel manager. Our room is still available—might as well take advantage of our honeymoon reservations while I'm here—all bought and paid for."

"Brad…now isn't the time." Marcia glanced his way.

He waited for her to tell her ex to go fly a kite. She didn't. He gritted his teeth as Holcomb continued.

"No, no, I insist. I'm sure the rest of our reservations are in place. I have several days to enjoy before we return. I've called a taxi. We'll be out of your hair before long. I talked with your P.I. here in Rio, and provided him with additional information you might be interested in. It's all about following the money. I'm glad I could be of help. Good luck with your business."

He'd had enough.

"If you'll excuse me, I have an important appointment. I'm sure *Marcie* will be more than happy to take care of you. Enjoy the rest of your stay here in Rio de Janeiro."

Jared glanced at Marcia before he walked inside the house, and out the front door. He had the key in the ignition, the motor running, and was down the drive in seconds.

****

She knew she should have spoken up in front of Jared before he walked out, but to what end? Letting him think she and Brad were back together…, well, Jared wasn't interested in her, or at least for the long term. The only thing it had done was encourage Bradley to think he was gaining ground in getting her back. She had to set him straight.

"Are you crazy?" Marcia confronted Brad, getting right up in his face and pointing her finger in his chest. "I'm not your fiancée, and I'm not going back to the hotel with you. Stay there if you want, but I don't want anything more to do with you. I told you—I don't love you."

"You can't be serious." He plunked his hands on his hips and threw his head back. "And here I flew all the way down to be with you, to apologize. To ask your forgiveness."

"For the love of Pete, Bradley, get over yourself. Go back to your lover."

"Give it time. I'm sure you'll see we're meant for each other."

Marcia shook her head. Was there nothing she could say or do to convince him she was serious that she didn't love him?

"I'm sorry, Brad. This is goodbye. I appreciate that you acted pro-bono on the family's behalf in order to clear Russell's name, but even so, it isn't enough to sway my feelings for you at this point. And I'm sorry if you really did come all this way thinking we were going to get back together."

"I'm sorry, too." He took her hands, held them at arm's length, and looked into her eyes. "Can we at least be friends—I really do care for you, and I am seriously sorry."

"I'm seriously sorry, too." She sighed, no longer upset with him. He'd done her a favor by helping to get Russell off the hook for being accused of stealing Jared's prototypes. But she had to admit she'd never really loved Brad enough to marry him—not if she could fall so easily into Jared's arms so soon after leaving Brad's.

What did that say about her?

"Before you go, can you at least tell me one thing? Are you one hundred percent sure the anonymous donation came from Jared's company account?"

He looked at her with pity in his mesmerizing eyes and then blinked as if he'd made up his mind about something.

"Yes. It was given with the express stipulation the name would never be revealed."

"How did you find out?"

"Ah, now, I would be giving away all my secrets and my sources. I never give away information about my contacts except if asked by a court of law. And even then I'd have to make a judgment call. Unless Russell has access to the accounts, I'd say this exonerates him on all charges. Someone else within the company is out to get Jared Reed. He might want to check his right-hand man. He wasn't very forthcoming when I contacted him. It's all about following the money."

"Have you told Jared what you discovered?"

"Not yet. But I talked to the P.I. he hired down here—a Marcelo Costas. I'm sure once he meets with him, he'll find out. I'm sure that's where he's headed now. I'll be at our hotel. If you change your mind, or need me for anything, give me a call. Are you sure you won't change your mind and come back with me?"

A horn beeped out front. Marcia shook her head and stepped aside.

"Your taxi is waiting. Thanks for your help with Russell. Please send us a bill."

"Not happening. It's the least I can do for all the hurt I've caused you. I'm truly sorry, Marcia."

"Goodbye, Brad."

He hesitated, hopeful she'd change her mind—she didn't back down. Tears threatened—tears for what might have been. Not with her and Bradley, but between her and Jared.

The taxi honked again. Brad nodded, and then walked away. He climbed into the taxi without a backward glance. The cab sped down the drive, into the street, and disappeared. She sank into one of the cushioned wicker chairs, and leaned her head back on the edge. And let the tears flow.

****

"Jared, this is the P.I. we hired—Marcelo Costas."

Jared shook the man's hand. "Pleased to meet you. Mr. Holcomb tells me he shared information with you and that you've uncovered additional information which might be helpful."

"Yes. Apparently, a Mr. Osaka has a company that buys and sells high-end DVD games such as yours. He has an office in downtown Rio. We have another client who hired us to keep an eye on Osaka, as well. Seems they are having the same problem as you. Two men worked with one of their technicians as a go-between with this Mr. Osaka—Ricardo Esposito and Paul Díaz. Minor criminals at best. We don't think they are capable of doing the kind of damage Mr. Kline sustained. In fact, these two were rather easy to locate. The authorities have apprehended them for questioning already. They were more than willing to squeal on this Mr. Rose. Who, by the way, has been very elusive until your American P.I., Mr. Holcomb, shared a picture of your Mr. Johnson with us this morning. The two men identified him as Mr. Rose without delay."

Jared cringed. Marcia was right. Hank was covering his ass by framing Russell. But why?

"I'm sorry." Kurt placed a hand on Jared's shoulder and gave it a sympathetic pat.

"So am I." Jared hung his head and shook it. His hair hung over his forehead. He brushed it aside. "I can't fathom why he would do such a thing. He's well paid. Hell, we've been friends since grade school. Are you certain it's Hank?"

Marcelo drew a photograph from his briefcase and placed it on the table in front of Jared and Kurt.

"*Dammit.*"

"There is more. Mr. Holcomb suggested we check into your own finances. It seems he's had access to your banking accounts and was the one who issued a sizable check to the church that held the benefit for Russell's family."

Jared sat down before his knees could give out. Kurt handed him a glass of brandy—he took it, threw it back automatically, shut his eyes, and pressed his lips together.

"We have word Mr. Johnson is on his way to Rio. I have informed the police. They have put a watch for him at all the local airports. If he comes into town on a plane, they have been instructed to follow him in hopes he will lead the authorities to Mr. Osaka. They will wait for money to exchange hands before they make an arrest."

"Please, let me know when he lands."

"What do you plan to do?" Kurt eyed Jared, and held up the bottle.

Jared declined. Kurt poured a shot for himself.

"Find out what the hell is going on. He owes me that much. The man has been running my business into the ground. I want to know why."

"It is best if you wait. You do not want to alarm him and make him run, as you say. Once he meets with Mr. Osaka, and we have them in custody, you will have a chance to speak with him."

"You're right, of course."

In the meantime, he needed to talk to Marcia. To apologize. It might be too late. She might already be in Holcomb's bed, but the least he could do is make amends for doubting her, especially after everything her brother had been through on his behalf. Everything she'd been through to try and clear his name. Admit she was right about Hank, and that Russell had only been trying to clear his name. And Hank? *Shit.* He might have stolen from the company, but at least the money had gone to a good cause. He hoped Russell's daughter's health was improving.

****

The antiseptic, bleach, and floor wax odors hit Jared the minute the hospital doors switched open. He had arranged for Russell to have a private room once he'd been taken out of I.C.U. He had made it clear Russell was to have a room with a view overlooking the beach. It was the least he could do.

He nodded to the two officers stationed outside the room. He wasn't taking any chances. He also arranged for a 24/7 guard. If the thugs who had done this to Russell were aware he was still alive, they might be back to finish the job. And until they were captured and put behind bars along with Hank and this Osaka character, the least he could do was make sure Russell's life was protected.

He stepped inside and paused. Marcia stood next to the window, her back to the door. He hadn't expected to find her here, at least not without Bradley Holcomb by her side. Lost for words, he scanned the room. Russell was propped up in bed, eyes closed, his skin tone not quite as pale as when he'd seen him last. All the tubes had been removed, including the I.V., and the swelling around his bruises weren't as pronounced. Thank God the man was on the mend from his ordeal. At least on the outside.

Either Marcia hadn't heard him come in, or she decided to ignore him. He took a deep breath, let it out, and rounded the foot of Russell's bed.

"Marcia?"

She swiveled to face him. Her head shot up, her eyes widened. Dammit. Tears streaked her pale face.

"Jared," she whispered.

He saw rather than heard his name on her lips. He wanted to kiss those tempting lips, but they weren't his to kiss—he had no right. The urge to run to her side, wrap his arms around her, and tell her he was sorry tugged at his heart. His feet remained planted next to the hospital bed.

Russell showed no indication he was aware he had a hospital room full of company.

"Will you come outside with me so we can talk?"

She hesitated. *Damn.* She wasn't going to give him an inch. She surprised him, however, and walked past him without a word. He was right behind her as she entered the cold, antiseptic corridor. He followed her to the waiting area at the end of the hall. The small cozy room was empty. Marcia sat on the small divan as if her legs wouldn't hold her another moment longer. She covered her face with her hands, her shoulders sagged, and she hung her head.

"Is it Russell?" He sat down next to her, wanting to take her in his arms and comfort her, dry her tears. "I thought he was taken off the critical list now that he has been moved out of I.C.U. Has that changed?"

She sniffed, sat back, and rested her head on the cushion, focusing on anything but him.

"No. Nothing has changed. He's improving and is going to be fine. Thank you for all you've done. The entire family appreciates it."

He ran his hand through his hair. *Shit.* How could he make this right for her? And, where the hell was Holcomb? The man should be here. By her side. Taking care of her.

"I've made arrangements for Russell's wife and daughter to fly down to be with him while he's in the hospital recuperating, and to have a few days holiday while they're here."

"I'm not sure Heather is well enough to fly."

"I've arranged for my private jet to fly them down,

along with your sister and her husband—if he wishes. They'll be more comfortable on my jet than on a commercial flight. I've arranged for them to stay at Kurt and Sophia's. You know Sophia—she'll welcome their company and pamper Heather no end."

"You don't need to do this."

"Russell will heal faster with his family by his side. After this ordeal, and their daughter's health issues, an extended break will do them all a world of good."

"They aren't your responsibility."

"It's the least I can do. And I owe you an apology. I should have listened to you. Trusted you. Russell was not only trying to clear his name, but he was trying to find out who was selling me out."

"Jared…"

He put his hands up to stop her. "Please. It's a done deal. I know Sophia will be happy to have them stay with her. And you're welcome to visit them whenever you wish. You won't have to worry about running in to me—I'm heading back to the Double R. I have a business to put back in order, and a ranch that needs my attention now the police have things under control down here—or will have before long. They've put undercover agents at all the airports. When Hank lands, they'll arrest him."

"Jared…"

"Please. You don't have to say a thing. I wish you all the best."

He couldn't resist. He leaned over, gave her a light kiss on her forehead, and walked away. His heart stopped beating. He held his breath, grabbed his chest, and kept walking down the hall. He'd survive. He always did.

Chapter Thirteen

"You try to swindle me. Send me fake prototype. You think I am stupid?"

"I didn't try to swindle you. I have the real prototype. I flew down to give it to you in person."

"Why should I believe you? The man you sent in your place got what he deserved. No one makes a fool of Osaka and gets away. You included."

Hank relaxed his eyes, his lips, and smiled. He wasn't about to let this man intimidate him or take advantage of his home turf. He panned the man's swanky office. It was evident by the expensive trappings that the man was good at what he did. The view overlooking Rio was spectacular. He waited another silent moment, giving Mr. Osaka a chance to wonder what he was up to before he spoke.

"If you don't want the prototype, say so. I'll find someone more than willing to pay the price. You are not the only fish in the pond."

"How can I trust there will not be any repercussions? I understand this Mr. Kline who pretended to represent you is alive. He has no doubt talked to the police. I think I do not take your deal."

Ready to call the man's bluff and walk away, Hank rose to leave. He needed Osaka's money, otherwise his dreams would be on hold. Of course, there were others ready to get on board. His contacts in Santiago were waiting in the wings. But that was going to take time to negotiate. With the way things were going, he didn't have time to waste.

"You have nothing to lose," he told Osaka. "Once you copy the files, make it your own, and destroy the original, you are free and clear. There is no trail to follow."

"So sorry. It is too late. I no longer wish to deal with you. Please. See yourself out."

"You think this is the end of our agreement? You think there will be no repercussions on your end once I walk out your door? I understand they've apprehended Ricardo and Paul."

"They are small time nobodies. No one will believe their lies."

"I don't need them to convince the authorities. I have proof they'd love to get their hands on in regards to Reed's avatar prototypes."

"You dare to threaten me?"

Mr. Osaka stood abruptly, leaned on his desk, and spread his fingertips on top—knuckles white. His eyes bulged with anger.

"I think you know better." Hank remained calm and tapped his finger on the table, for emphasis. "If we do not have a deal, then we are finished. There will be no other offers on the table from me in future. I'll give you until this afternoon to think things over. If I don't hear from you by five o'clock, I will sell to someone else. Your choice."

"Do not hold your breath, as you Americans say. Goodbye, *Mr. Rose.*"

Hank smiled. No way was he going to let this Jap get the better of him. He nodded, bowed, then backed out the door, never taking his eyes off Mr. Osaka. Once out of the man's sight, he made a mad dash out of the building and around the corner to his car. Congratulating himself he was no longer connected with Mr. Osaka, and was free to make contact with his other buyers before he was discovered, he punched in Jared's speed dial number. It was time to find out what Jared knew about Ricardo and Paul's arrest. Had the men squealed? Had they pointed the finger at him?

Phone to his ear, Hank didn't hear the two men come from behind until they surrounded him. They didn't waste any time latching onto his arms and frog-marching him back around the side of the building. His cell phone flew in the air, his feet slid out from under him, and he was slammed against the side of the building.

Dammit. Osaka's henchmen. He hadn't expected the punch to the stomach, the clip to the side of his head. The only thing keeping him from sliding to the pavement was the two meaty hands wrapped around his neck. He couldn't breathe. About to pass out from lack of oxygen, he was lifted, dragged, and thrown into a SUV—the doors already open and waiting. He wrestled away from them before they could tie his hands, or knock him senseless. He needed to be alert to strategize his plan of escape. He assumed these were the two men who had beaten the crap out of Russell and left him for dead. Which meant, they wouldn't be too concerned about keeping him alive, either.

Once inside the van, the driver stepped on the gas, and the vehicle shot out into the traffic while the taller of the two men threw him to the floor, rolled him onto his stomach none too gently, and tied his hands behind his back. As he was about to kick backwards to throw his attacker off course, the heavy-set thug plunked down on his legs and quickly had them tied together with a strong plastic zip-tie. The man vaulted over the seat and joined the driver in the front. If his captors thought he wouldn't be able to break out of the plastic, they were crazy. One swift yank of his legs, and he'd be free. These men weren't as smart as they were dumb— it was going to be a cinch to escape, given the chance.

The vehicle jerked sideways sending him flying. He landed to the side of the van with a thud. The car swerved to the right, he rolled to the other side of the van. Tires squealed. The vehicle bumped up over a curb, then took off like a shot again. Left alone in the back, Hank held his breath, kicked his feet apart, and split the zip-tie open. At least his feet were free. Propping his back against the side of the van, he searched for something sharp to cut the nylon rope on his hands. These guys weren't any too neat. Empty coffee cups, carry-out trays, and dirty wrappers littered the back. Electrical equipment, wires, tools, and a metal box were secured along the other side of the van. He scanned the upper area and spotted two semi-automatic guns strapped to the ceiling. *Holy shit!* These guys were way more dangerous than he credited. For the first time he wondered where they were taking him. If they were going to shoot him first chance they got. He needed to get out of there—the sooner the better.

Not finding anything sharp to use to free his hands, he inched his way to the back of the van next to the double doors. The car picked up speed. The two men in the front seat yelled and cussed at each other in Portuguese. Sirens blared in the distance. Coming closer and closer—louder. Lights flashed. *Shit.* They were emergency bar lights on top of a police vehicle. The police stuck close to the van, turn for turn. Hank lay back against the side of the interior, and braced his body with his feet. The car weaved in and out of traffic. His stomach lurched. Hell, he was going to vomit if this kept up.

The van's breaks squealed, and the car careened sideways, slamming up against a stone wall, scraped for several yards. It rocked back and forth, teetered on end, and then tipped over on its side. Hank bounced around in the van like a rag doll. Unable to protect his head, the final impact knocked him out cold.

****

Jared pulled in the drive and got out of his car. Kurt met him at the front door.

"We have to talk."

"What's up?" He didn't like the apprehensive expression on his brother's face. "Is Marcia okay? There hasn't been another attempt to kidnap her, has there?"

"No. But they've apprehended Hank."

Jared followed his brother in the front door, through the house, out the back door, and sat on the edge of one of the wicker patio chairs.

"Okay. Let's have it. What aren't you telling me?"

"Apparently, Hank flew commercial into Sâo Paulo. The authorities put a tail on him, as promised, hoping he would lead them to Mr. Osaka. He did. But before they could step in and arrest them both, Osaka's henchmen shoved Hank into a van and took off. They gave chase for several blocks. The vehicle knocked into a couple of garbage cans, sent a fruit vendor flying, and

180

hit a couple of people walking along the street before they crashed, and rolled over."

"Oh, my God! Is Hank dead? What about the others?"

"No. Thankfully, no one was killed. But Hank and the driver were pretty banged up from the accident. They transported them to the hospital for treatment and have been released. Hank and the other two have been arrested and taken to jail. Luckily the bystanders didn't sustain major injuries, and were released, as well."

"What about Osaka?"

"He got away. Marcelo told me the police have leads they are following. Putting a 'no fly' status on him so he doesn't leave the country."

"What about the borders? He probably has contacts willing to help him cross over."

"We can't worry about that right now. The police assured Marcelo they'd handle it at this point."

"This makes no sense. What in the hell was Hank thinking?"

Jared leaned back in his seat, heaved a deep sigh, and shook his head.

"How did I not see this?"

"Sorry. Don't know what else I can say. At least we broke up the deal. You aren't completely ruined."

"Maybe I should give up the technology business and stick with ranching."

"You've worked too hard on both all your life, and doing a commendable job at it."

"That's the problem—it's become my whole life. I've let so much pass me by, I'm beginning to wonder if it's all been worth it."

"What about Marcia?"

"What about her? She's gone back to her fiancé."
"I'm not so sure. Maybe you should talk to her."
"To what end? I'd be wasting my time."
"Chicken shit!"
"You could be right—for once in your life."

****

Instead of talking to Marcia, Jared drove to the jail to see Hank—find out what the hell he'd been thinking. Find out what had gone wrong.

Jared ran his shaking fingers through his already disheveled hair, and stared at his friend. Hank's blank glare was arctic, made even meaner by the shiner having become an ugly black and blue. His cheek was cut and held together with two wide butterfly bandages. His left arm was in a sling, and a stretch bandage was wrapped firmly around his right foot and ankle. Jared shook his head. Who was this man sitting on the other side of the cold steel bars?

"Why? My God, Hank. We've been friends and partners since we were kids in grade school. What the hell went wrong?"

"Friends? Hell, I've been nothing but your lapdog all these years. Second best all the way—girls, school, college, sports, even in business."

"It was never a competition. We've always been equals."

"As far as you're concerned maybe. But you've had everything—a successful company, one of the biggest spreads in the state of Oregon. And you don't even appreciate any of it, damn you. You haven't had to work for any of it. Your family handed it to you on a silver platter as if it were your due."

"Are you crazy? I've worked my ass off to get

where I am today. As for the Double R—you know it wasn't just handed to me. I had a hell of a time keeping it in the family and making it a prosperous endeavor after my grandfather and father passed."

"If it weren't for me and the others you wouldn't be where you are, raking in the millions with your precious avatar games."

"You don't think I don't know that? I've made sure each and every one of you were handsomely compensated—every step of the way. You, of all people should understand how hard that's been."

Hank's face contorted in a pinched, sinister expression. Jared stepped back. He took a good hard look at his friend and wondered when their friendship had gone sour.

"How long have you felt this way?"

"Are you kidding? I've wanted to get out from under your hold on me from the start. I've scrimped and saved and worked my ass off for you until I could get enough capital to form my own company. And I was about ready to break away when Russell started snooping around."

"So you decided to frame him instead? Why Russell?"

"What? Mr. Goody-two-shoes? Like I said, he started snooping around. Getting too close to what I was doing. I had to do something. It wasn't hard to pull the reports together."

"Excuse me! You pulled the reports together by yourself? I thought you had a P. I. checking into the case." Jared gritted his teeth. The S.O.B. had lied about that, too.

"It wasn't hard to do. The church benefit opened

up his records to the public so people would donate."

"And on top of that, you had Russell beaten and left for dead? How does it feel?"

Hank slumped back on the jail cell cot like he owned it.

"I intercepted a letter he sent to you while you were in Rio. He implicated me—wanted you to check me out. I couldn't take the chance that you would find out."

Jared stood, feet spread apart, hands in his pants pockets staring at his longtime friend. Hank looked up at him through a half-closed swollen eye. He certainly didn't look like his friend at the moment.

"I didn't ask them to beat up on Russell, or leave him for dead. I had nothing to do with their actions. Osaka took matters into his own hands when he thought Russell was double-crossing him. Ricardo and Paul were only supposed to scare him away. Get him to back off."

"You don't think Russell and his family haven't suffered enough? His daughter had a relapse and has been back in the hospital while he's been down here attempting to clear his name. A name you've dragged through hell, I might add. What in God's name were you thinking? He should have been by her side. Not only did you put Russell's life in danger, Marcia has been through hell on her brother's behalf. They ransacked her room, they attempted to kidnap her, and they set her up to literally take a fall and kill her on Sugar Loaf yesterday. I had to zip-line the both of us down off the damn thing. Luckily, I had my leather belt with the wide silver buckle. Dammit, we almost didn't make it down before they cut the cable."

Jared paced in front of Hank's cell pod, hands fisting. He wanted to punch Hank and blacken his other eye.

Hank hung his head. Good. The man should feel guilty. He was fortunate there were bars separating them.

"You're lucky Russell is going to make it—at least you won't be an accessory to murder. Why? Why did you do this? It's bad enough you were running my business into the ground, but you also stole money from one of my accounts. What went wrong, Hank? Do you hate me that much?"

Jared flew too many questions at Hank at once. He didn't care. His mind buzzed with them. Nothing made sense. He didn't think it ever would.

"I planned to put the money back as soon as I closed this deal with the Japs. I was aware it would make Russell look guilty. But if it's any consolation, my heart went out to him and his family. Losing Rosemary early on to cancer, I knew the devastating effect it had on those left behind. A child has to be hard to bury—never mind a wife. Thankfully, we never had any children. Anyway, once Osaka handed over the money, I was going to pay you back. If that damn P.I. from New York hadn't come snooping around, the money would have been returned already, and no one the wiser."

"But you inherited a ton of money from your in-laws when Rosemary died. What happened to it?"

"You think I didn't have a ton of medical bills because of Rosemary's cancer. Man, insurance only covered so much. And then there were all those treatments, year after year. In and out of the hospital.

And there wasn't as much as you think after her parent's debts were paid off. Believe me, they left a few. I was broke by the time I buried my wife."

Jared finally put two and two together—the Rose—Rosemary. Hank's dead wife's name? Why hadn't he made the connection sooner? Maybe it was because he had never considered Hank the one selling him out. If it wasn't for Marcia's sister hiring Holcomb, they might never have uncovered the truth about the money Hank had withdrawn from the company's account. Hank had certainly made sure he kept that crucial piece of information to himself.

"The ironic thing is, Hank, I would have been more than happy to help you get started on your own if you'd confided in me like the friends I considered we were. As for helping to set you up in your own company—hell, there's a lot of room out there for our kind of technology. You didn't need to sell it out from under me."

"And be beholden to you one more time? No thanks."

Jared shook his head, a big piece of his childhood—his life, died inside. His best friend had tried to run him into the ground. But a friend, nevertheless. He might regain control of his company and the falling sales, but he lost something more precious—his best friend and the woman he loved. Not able to look at Hank a moment longer, he turned his back on his longtime friend. He nodded to the guard to escort him down the hall and out into the fresh air.

It was time to set things right with Russell.

And Marcia.

Chapter Fourteen

"Glad to see you awake. You look much better than the last time I visited. How are you feeling?" Jared pulled up a chair and sat next to Russell's bed.

"I think I'm going to live. Although, I wasn't sure there for a while. I'm sorry about your avatar prototypes. I thought I could figure out who was responsible for selling them, but I guess I'm not that great a sleuth after all." Russell smiled, leaned over and accepted Jared's handshake, then settled back in his hospital bed.

"I'm the one who's sorry, man. I had no idea what was going on behind my back. Guess I don't have the control, or the people skills I need to run the business and figure out I was being stabbed in the back. Obviously, trying to run two businesses at the same time wasn't working out as great as I assumed."

"It wouldn't have made any difference. Any idea who wanted to see you fail?"

"To be honest, I had a hard time believing it was you. However, with the information Hank handed me, it made you look guilty as hell. I had no reason not to believe him."

Jared shook his head, sighed. He hated to admit it was his best friend. How had he missed all the signs? They'd practically lived out of each other's pockets since childhood—they were that close.

"I've got to ask," Russell paused, blinked, and then continued, "was it Hank?"

Jared nodded, unable to voice Russell's correct assumption. His gut ached picturing his best friend behind bars. Listening to him, Hank hadn't had an ounce of regret in him. Jared shook his head.

"Yes. It was Hank. Thanks to Marcia's fiancé we were able to figure it out. Holcomb was quite helpful in investigating our own P.I. Which, I'm ashamed to say, turned out to be a hoax. Hank assembled all the reports he presented to me."

"I'm sorry, Jared. This must be hard for you to accept. You and Hank go back a long way. It's hard to come to terms with something like this when you've invested so much faith in a person."

"You have no idea. I'm still shaking my head. I understand you sent me a letter warning me it might be Hank. Unfortunately, he intercepted it after I left for Rio. I'm not so sure I would have given it a second thought if I'd been the one to open it. Now…I'm the one who's sorry. It's my fault you've been through so much. And I aim to fix it."

"Not necessary, as long as I still have a job with your company."

"Hell, yes. No question. Your position is secure for as long as you want it. The question is, do you want the job not knowing what the fallout is going to be with our foreign connections?"

"I don't imagine it will take long for them to jump back on the wagon—if they've even started bailing. Unless you've been informed otherwise, Argentina, Chile, and Brazil are very interested in working with Reed Technologies."

"Still are. I met with them yesterday. Wanted to see if they'd heard from you since you arrived in Rio. They had nothing but glowing things to say on your behalf."

Russell's skin tones notched up a shade.

"It's good to hear." He relaxed his head and shoulders into the pillow.

"Listen, I don't want you to worry about a thing. Hank and the thugs who attacked you and left you for dead are behind bars. The company will pay your hospital and medical expenses. I'll see your daughter's medical expenses are covered, as well. As for making it easier for you to stop worrying about them, I've made my jet available to fly them down here to be with you. They should arrive later this evening."

Tears formed in Russell's eyes. He wiped at them with the back of his hands, not ashamed to cry. Jared swallowed, and shut his own eyes tight before he could gain control of his voice. He cleared his throat.

"I've already made arrangements for them to stay at Kurt's. I know they'll be more comfortable and well taken care of at their place. Your sister Samantha and her husband were invited to accompany them if they wish."

"You don't need to do this, Jared. You've already done enough giving me my job back."

"You never lost your job. Besides, it's the least I can do—you almost lost your life trying to save my company. In fact, I'm sure you deserve a promotion. Expect one when you get back to the states."

On his way out of the hospital Jared called ahead to have his jet ready to take him back to Oregon as soon as Russell's wife and daughter landed. He needed to put his life back in order. Well, his business, anyway.

He'd never felt less excited about anything in his life. Or more lonely.

****

Marcia entered the hospital as Jared was leaving.

"How's Russell?" She stepped aside giving Jared access to the door.

"Russell is doing okay. I've filled him in about Hank."

"How did he take it?"

"He wasn't surprised. Seems I'm the only one who was unaware of what was going on under my nose."

"Trust me, it happens."

"Do you have a minute before you go up to see your brother? I could use a coffee in the cafeteria."

"Well…"

"Please. I'd like a word."

Marcia followed him to the busy cafeteria. She found a table next to the window while Jared went through the line to get their coffee. What did he have to talk to her about? She twisted a strand of hair and tucked it behind her ear. She should have pulled it back in a French twist to get it off her neck in this heat, but she'd been too frustrated and in a hurry. She had hoped to avoid meeting Jared.

"I brought you a cheese Danish. I hope you like it."

"Thanks."

He slid the tray on the table and sat, then lifted a cup to those tantalizing lips. Her heart picked up a beat. Would she ever be able to get the taste of his lips out of her mind? She sipped at her coffee, and then took a bite of the Danish. She was sure it was delicious, but it tasted like cardboard.

"I owe you an apology—for doubting you. And for

thinking you were involved is this mad scheme."

"You don't have to do this. I understand. After all, there was no proof that I wasn't involved—or Russell, for that matter. You have a company to protect. It's not your fault your right-hand man filled you full of crap."

"You're right. Hank filled me full of crap. But it's my fault I believed him. I doubted Russell could be involved. I should have trusted my instincts. I should have insisted I talk to Hank's P.I. I would have discovered the man didn't exist."

What could she say? She filled the silence by biting into her pastry and gulping down coffee she no longer wanted.

"I'm sorry, Marcia. About everything. About us."

"Don't, Jared. I'm the one to apologize for letting 'us' happen. I got caught up in the whole Rio *Carnaval* atmosphere, the dance, the music, the craziness—it's contagious."

He sat back, put his coffee cup back on the tray, and looked out the window.

"As I said earlier, I made arrangements for your sister-in-law and niece to come to Rio to be by Russell's side while he heals. I've invited your sister and her husband to join them. I've sent my jet back to fly them in. They should be arriving later this evening."

"Jared…"

"Hear me out. I informed Russell that Reed Technologies is picking up his hospital tab. It's the least I can do for all he's gone through on my behalf. And flying his family down here is not a problem. I'll need the jet to fly back to the ranch to put my company back in order. I have to see about hiring a new technical assistant. And for various reasons, someone to keep an eye on my accounts."

Marcia's insides stilled. He was leaving. She knew he had a business and ranch to run. She smiled through stiff lips and nodded. What had she expected—a plea of undying love?

"If you'd like, I'll pick you up and drive you to the airport so you can meet them when they arrive. Unless you'd rather your fiancé take you."

"I'd appreciate a lift to the airport. I'll meet you at Sophia's. Thanks."

****

The tension inside Jared's car as they drove to the airport closed in on her. Marcia's chest ached knowing he was on his way back to Oregon—and out of her life forever.

"It's very generous of you to fly Russell's family down to be with him. You didn't need to."

For someone who didn't want to be tied down, he was showing a family side of him that surprised her. The man had a heart after all. Too bad there wasn't room for her in one of those compartments.

"Like I said, it's the least I can do after what Russell went through on my behalf. Don't make me out to be something I'm not, Marcia. I have a business to run. Having Russell's family by his bedside will help him heal faster. It's good business. The sooner he gets back on his feet, the sooner he's back on the job."

So much for his heart of gold.

"I'm sure they appreciate the opportunity to be by his side. Although, they would have been just as happy staying at a small hotel. You didn't need to impose on Kurt and Sophia. They don't need the extra responsibility of Heather's health issues."

"Now that you've moved back to the hotel with Brad, there's plenty of room. You know Sophia—she'll love the company."

She wasn't about to correct his wrong assumption that she was joining Brad at the hotel. Let him think what he wanted. He was leaving her behind and going back to Oregon. Once again, he was putting his business ahead of a relationship. He didn't need the complications of another person tying him down. End of story.

She'd been a fool once again to think Jared might care enough to ask her to go back to Oregon with him.

The rest of the drive to the airport was accomplished in silence. Jared dropped her off in front of the terminal, and drove off to park the car. By the time he rejoined her, her sister Sammie was ushering Bea and Heather, who was in a wheelchair, through customs. Within seconds of them seeing each other, they were all in each other's arms.

"Where is Mark? Didn't he come with you?"

"No. He's working on a contract and couldn't get away."

"How was the flight? Did Heather do okay?"

"Yes. She slept most of the time, but she's doing great. Excited to visit Rio. What about you? I'm so sorry, Marcia. I know you've gone through hell while you've been down here on your own." Sammie brushed the hair out of her eyes and tucked it behind her ear. "I didn't anticipate it would be this serious. But if there was anyone able to handle it, it was you. You're stronger than the rest of us."

Marcia gave Sammie's arm a tight squeeze. "Thanks, I'm doing okay." She didn't feel strong at all.

Right now she had all to do to keep her legs from dropping out from under her.

"At least Russell is alive and out of harm's way."

"Have they arrested that evil man?"

"Hank? Yes. We'll talk later. Let's get Bea and Heather taken care of first. They look ready to crash."

"We had a lovely ride in Mr. Reed's jet, didn't we Heather?" Bea smiled, hugging Marcia, again. "Heather slept most of the way. The ride was very comfortable."

Marcia bent down to give her niece a warm but gentle hug, and a peck on her cheek.

"All the more reason to settle Heather in as soon as we can. We don't want her to get too fatigued."

"All this bright sunshine and the warm tropical breeze will help her tremendously. A few days of relaxing on the beach will do her good." Bea glanced over Marcia's shoulder. A smile lit her face. "Mr. Reed. Thanks so much for giving us the opportunity to be by Russell's side in his time of need. It's very gracious of you."

"Think nothing of it. Glad to help. I've instructed the car rental department to provide you with a small SUV during your stay. You can pick up the keys at the rental desk. Give them my name. It's paid for." He held his hand out to Marcia. "Here are the keys to my rental. I've extended it in your name. You can use it until you leave."

Marcia didn't know when he'd had a chance to make all these arrangements, but marveled at his generosity.

"If you ladies will excuse me, I have a jet to catch."

He might have been talking to the group standing in front of him, but his eyes locked with hers. She couldn't read his mind behind those cold searching eyes. Her heart sank. This was it. The end. Once again it was over before it began.

"Walk with me."

Not waiting for agreement, he slipped his arm around her shoulders and led her to a secluded corner away from the cavernous space filled with tourists. The alcove was hidden away from passengers as they scurried to and fro in a hurry to get to their own destinations.

He gazed into her eyes again, his masked. She waited, wanting him to take her into his arms, kiss her, and tell her he couldn't live without her. But he didn't. She ached to throw her arms around his neck, kiss him, and beg him to stay. She didn't. She held back knowing he didn't want the commitment she craved. Forever-after be damned—she'd take whatever he offered. For however long it lasted.

He leaned in. Her heart raced. She lifted her face in expectation of his kiss. Her eyes shut in anticipation. His lips connected in a quick, tepid peck on her forehead. He released her, and left without saying a word. She staggered, gripped the wall behind her for support and could only stare at his back as he retreated, disappearing through the crowd.

Her heart stopped. Tears gathered. Blinded by an overwhelming desire to disappear from the crowd, she quickly ducked into the nearest ladies' room, slid into the closest stall, and locked herself behind closed doors. And let the tears flow. *Dammit.* She had to get her act together. Sammie, Bea, and Heather were waiting outside. They didn't need any more of her tearful theatrics. She couldn't let them see what a sap she'd become over Jared Reed. Having recently been made a fool of by Brad, she wasn't about to elicit any more of their sympathy. Nope. She was going to go out there and shake it off and act as if she was enjoying Rio de Janeiro and all it had to offer. Show how happy she was that they were all together—Russell was going to mend—and that she didn't have a care in the world.

She sighed. *Yeah. Right.* Sammie would see right through her the minute she walked out the door. She sniffed. Snatched some tissue from the roll, wiped her tear-stained face, blew her nose, threw the tissue in the bowl, and flushed the toilet. It was time to pull up her big girl panties and face life without Jared. She stood in front of the mirror. *Gad, she looked pathetic.* She reached into her purse and pulled out her maroon makeup bag. She rinsed her face, refreshed her makeup, took a deep breath, and exited the busy facility.

Sammie gave her the eye the minute she spotted her. Marcia shook her head, pasted a smile on her face, and walked through the frenzied mob. Three more days. She had three more days left in Rio. She should be happy and take advantage of the time she had left, but instead wished she was flying back to Oregon with Jared.

"You all right?" Sammie gave her a knowing look.

"Never better. Let's get Bea and Heather out of this crowded terminal and into the bright tropical sunshine. It will do Heather a world of good."

"Never better, my foot. You know you can't hide your feelings from me."

"I'll be okay, Sam. You know me. I always bounce back."

They followed Bea and Heather through the

terminal, keeping an eye on them, making sure they didn't encounter any difficulty with the wheelchair.

"I don't want to put a damper on Bea and Heather's holiday, however short. Or yours. They have enough on their plate already, and you know how Bea worries about everyone else but herself. She needs this break. I don't want to ruin it for them. They deserve some fun."

Marcia walked Sammie to the car rental area where Sammie retrieved the keys. Together they helped Heather into the car.

"I'll return the wheelchair, and meet you back at the hospital. Will you be all right driving in this traffic?"

"I'm used to traffic. Besides, we have the GPS to help us find the way. We'll be okay."

Marcia hugged each of them, then faced Sammie. "Be careful. Even though *Carnaval* is almost over, it's still in progress and there's a bunch of crazies out there—day and night."

"Got it. See you later."

After returning the wheelchair to the airport, Marcia made her way back to the car park where Jared had left his car. How was she ever going to spend the next three days in Rio without thinking about Jared? His presence surrounded her—it was in the breeze, the vista, the surf, and the sand. Looking at Sugar Loaf Mountain had her libido tingling with the emotions of how her body had reacted to his on their snug and erotic zip-line ride down to safety. They'd been through so much together trying to figure out who framed Russell. Not to mention the breathtakingly romantic night they'd spent on the beach. How was she ever going to erase that night from her mind?

Marcia depressed the automatic key fob to unlock the car door when a restraining hand landed on her arm. Startled, she whipped around, raised her other hand in self-defense only to find Brad stepping back, brows raised.

"It's only me, Marcie."

She sighed and visibly relaxed. He dropped his hand.

"Guess I'm still on the alert after what those thugs have put me and Russell through."

He drew her in close. She let him. He rubbed soothing, firm hands over her back. Wanting to relax and let bygones be bygones, she sighed, swallowed, and then fought the urge to give him something to cling on to. And failed. She stepped away. No matter how hard she tried, passionate and tender feelings for Brad just weren't there. Had they ever been? Had it always been about being in love with the idea of marriage and having a family of her own?

"Thanks for all your help in clearing Russell's name."

"My pleasure. I did it for you. For us. It's my way of proving to you how much I care for you."

He looked deep into her eyes. He didn't see what he longed to see because it wasn't there. She lowered her head, backed out of his space and sighed.

"You don't know how much I regret my actions, Marcie. I hope someday you can find it in your heart to forgive me. Someday soon. I miss you. Can't you find it in your heart to forgive me?"

"You need to forgive yourself, and take responsibility for your actions if you ever want a meaningful relationship."

He kissed her then, a deep, heartfelt kiss. Marcia wished it was Jared who held her in his arms instead of Brad. She untangled his arms and let out a deep breath.

"You'd better go before you miss your flight."

"I'd miss it for you..."

"Please, don't. This really is goodbye."

His smile wobbled, his lips formed a straight line. He nodded, and then made his way toward the terminal.

What was it about men walking away from her? Granted Brad's defection no longer bothered her, but watching his back reminded her of watching Jared's back as he had walked away from her minutes ago.

For the first time in days, she wondered if Wild and Wonderful would hire her back.

Chapter Fifteen

Jared climbed aboard his jet, nodded to his pilot, and then found his favorite seat in the back. He plunked down next to the window. The view outside the porthole didn't interest him at the moment. He leaned his head against the seat's soft fabric, and shut his eyes. Big mistake.

What a stupid moron he'd been to run back to talk to Marcia—to tell her what he'd wanted to say in the terminal before he stupidly walked away without a word. The sad, stunned look on her pale face almost had him snatching her up and carting her off to the Double R. God, she looked as if he'd broken her heart. He wanted to mend it. Tell her he loved her. Needed her. So much for wanting to take her in his arms, sweep her off her feet, and take her back to the ranch. The vision of making love to her in flight washed over him.

He rubbed his hands over his face, shut his eyes tight and groaned. It wasn't meant to be. He couldn't have been more wrong about Marcia's feelings for him. Her woebegone eyes almost had him convinced he was making a huge mistake by not taking her in his arms and kissing her senseless. Dammit, he shouldn't have bothered to stop his jet from taking off so he could go back to talk to her. Seeing her in Bradley Holcomb's arms in the parking lot, their lips locked together in an I'll-be-damned-I-want-you kiss had him stopping in his tracks. His heart had dropped clear to the pavement. Doing an about-face, he'd tucked his tail between his legs and ran back to his jet like a wounded hound. It was clear the two had made up and were in the throes of resuming their honeymoon.

He might have been able to salvage his business and the Double R, but losing his best friend, and his girl, all in one week wasn't the consolation prize he'd anticipated.

He'd screwed up, dammit. Seeing her to the airport to meet her family hadn't gone as planned, either. Leaving her in tears when he left the airport and not saying a single damn word wasn't the best move he'd ever made. Especially, with someone he cared for more than he wanted to admit. Shit. His love life was totally in the toilet. It was his own fault. He should have been forewarned. Seen it coming.

The flight back to Oregon was a long, lonely, restless one. Remembering the passion and how perfectly Marcia fit in his arms when they'd made love on the beach afforded little comfort. She'd completed him, fulfilled him. And left him wanting more. Much more. For once in his life he'd been on the edge of having it all. But he'd held back, and it was much too late. He'd been afraid to make a commitment until his business was back on solid ground. He'd forfeited so much over the years while trying to grow the business and make the Double R a viable proposition. Too many opportunities had passed him by. And damn it, when he was ready to rectify the situation, find time to get a real life and make a commitment—give his heart to another human being, instead of his life-long ambition to build an technology empire, it was too late.

He swallowed. Raked tense fingers thought his hair, pounded them on the arm rest, and tried to focus his blurry, unseeing eyes out the window.

How in hell was he ever going to live without her?

****

As soon as Marcia got back to Sophia's, she called Wild and Wonderful. Waiting for someone to pick up at the other end of the phone had her tapping her fingers on the end table. She'd beg for a job if she had to. Anticipating having to leave a message, she sighed and waited for the answering machine to click in. Instead, someone answered.

"Hello. This is Marcia Kline calling for Helen Maps. Is she in the office?"

"I'm sorry. Ms. Maps is unavailable right now. She's on a long-distance call to France. Can I give her a message?"

"Yes. Please tell her I called from Rio and would appreciate it if she returned my call."

Marcia gave her the number, and then hung up. So much for having a chance to beg.

An hour later, Sophia appeared to tell her she had a phone call from New York.

Yes! It had to be a good omen that Helen would call back so soon.

"Hi, Helen. Thanks for calling back. I wanted to touch base and see if there was any chance that Wild and Wonderful had an opening."

"I have some things in the works, but nothing right now," Helen said. "What happened? I heard rumors that you called off your wedding. Is that true?"

"Yes. Unfortunately, you heard right. But I'm fine. Just need to find a job and an apartment so I don't have to move in with my sister and her husband."

"I'm so sorry to hear of your troubles. Perhaps if you call back in a couple months I could use your expertise. But it would require relocating. I'm in the process of opening another branch office overseas—either Eastern Europe or Asia. I've had several requests from both areas. If this is something you're interested in, I'll keep you posted."

At this point she'd relocate to Timbuktu if she had to.

****

Sophia's students twirled manically to the syncopated music, never missing a beat. Marcia smiled, laughed, and clapped with the rest of them. Her insides in turmoil, her head rumbled in time with the rhythm of the children's band. Would her heart ever mend? Two more days. That's all she had left of her time here in Rio de Janeiro. Two days to try to make it without her family realizing how miserable she was inside since Jared left. Keeping up the charade of being happy until she returned to New York only intensified the throbbing headache she'd woken up with that morning.

"Aunt Marcia, do you think Sophia will teach me how to dance like her students?" Heather had all to do to contain the excitement in her voice. It was good to see the sparkle in her eyes and the bright smile back on her face.

"I'm sure she would, but I think you need to recuperate a little longer before you exert that kind of energy."

"You will come back when you are feeling much better." Sophia stepped in and hugged Heather. "I will teach you. Your aunt will make sure you visit." She looked at Marcia for confirmation.

"Of course. Perhaps next year, when both you and your father are recovered, you can arrange a trip."

"That would be lovely." Bea hugged her daughter and leaned in to give her a quick peck on her forehead. "We will plan on it. You can help me with putting together an itinerary."

"Sophia, your students are amazing." Sammie joined them. "And the costumes these boys and girls are wearing…oh, my, they are simply spectacular. Such bold and brilliant colors. I especially love the bright tangerine with the solid green trim. And those burgundy and aqua feathers. Wow."

"A professional seamstress sews all our garments. I am so proud of my kids. They work very hard to be perfect."

"And so you should be. Do they compete at the big event?"

"No, they are too young to dance at *Carnaval*. They will be excellent dancers when older, then they will compete. Come, I will introduce you to my students."

Sophia led Heather and Bea into the frenzied throng of students moving and chatting, overly excited from their performance. Marcia held back, her headache worsening. Sammie stayed behind, as well.

"Are you okay? I get the feeling your heart isn't in any of this."

"I woke with a headache, and it's being persistent. But you're right. I can't pull the wool over your eyes, can I? You've always been able to see right through me."

"Yes. So what gives? Wait. Don't tell me. Let me

guess. Jared."

"I thought he had feelings for me, but I was wrong. His work is his life. He doesn't have time for a long-term relationship. And, I'm not looking for a short term love affair."

"Did he tell you he wasn't interested?"

"Oh, he's interested, but not in a forever-after. And, if you recall, he was the one who walked away, wasn't he?"

"Did you talk to him? Tell him you love him?"

"What? And be rebuffed again like I was two years ago. No, thanks. My heart can't take any more rejection from men who profess to love me, but don't."

Bea and Heather chose that moment to rejoin them, ending their conversation. Marcia smiled. Sammie smirked, and tisked.

"Heather and I decided to go to the hospital to visit Russell. Care to join us?" Bea jingled her car keys by her side.

"I'll drive you," Sammie offered. "How about you, Marcia? You want to ride along?"

"You go on without me. I think I'll head back and lie down for a while. See if I can get rid of this headache. Give Russell my love. Tell him I'll stop by later."

****

After she woke from her nap, Marcia went in search of Sophia, and found her sitting out on the patio.

"Come. Sit for a spell. It is too hot to cook. I think we take dinner cruise and enjoy the cool breezes tonight. Relax. Your family will enjoy. What do you say?"

Marcia's heart wasn't in it, but it was better than

sitting around moping all night.

"That's a lovely idea. Heather will love it."

"And you? You are too sad—such a pretty face. You do not smile. Your sister Samantha say you need a good man. A man like our Jared perhaps?"

"Yes, well, I want to thank you for inviting my family to stay with you instead of at a hotel. It's been a special treat for Bea and Heather. They don't often get to travel with Russell."

"We are happy to have them any time. But you change the topic. Call Jared. Talk to him. I think he is jealous. He believes you are in love with your P.I. you were engaged to marry."

Before Marcia had a chance to respond and confirm she no longer had feelings for Brad, Sammie strolled into the kitchen.

"What are you two cooking up?"

"We changed our minds." Sophia waved her hands in the air. "It is settled. We will all go on a dinner cruise tonight. Maybe then you can talk sense into your sister's head."

Marcia's brows rose. She put up her hands at the knowing look on Sammie's face.

"Don't start. It's bad enough Sophia is badgering me to run after Jared—I don't need you championing her side, too."

"What? I didn't say a word."

Marcia was saved once again as Bea and Heather appeared in the doorway.

"Can we help?" Bea asked.

"But of course. You can get ready, and we will go on a dinner boat tonight. We will enjoy."

"Is Kurt going with us?" Marcia walked around the

table on her way up to her room to get ready.

"He will be late tonight, so no, I am afraid not. He has an errand to do for his business. Come, you get ready. I will make the reservations and call the taxi."

Music blared from the boat as they walked up the gangway. Scantily sequined and glitzy dressed men and women in bold assorted colors, feathers and sequins assisted them once they boarded. Others, sporting elaborate gowns, massive headpieces covered with colorful feathers flouncing in the evening breeze like macaws ready to take flight, and strappy glittering matching heels, escorted them to their tables. They were taken to the middle deck and a corner table next to an open window affording them an excellent view of the shoreline, as well as the floor show. A long buffet table stretched down the center of the floor overflowing with hot and cold serving dishes. At the far end was a full bar already crowded with party-goers. Dinner was served almost immediately, and an hour later the buffet was dismantled and the evening entertainment began. Samba dancers barely dressed—skirts wound tight below their navels flowed down around stiletto strapped heels and brightly colored toenails, many of them were the waiters and waitresses who had greeted them when they boarded the ship. Skimpy pasties covered firm, glistening breasts in sequined baubles on a few, and neck and head pieces matched the barely-there outfits. Marcia wondered how in the world they managed to keep everything on while rapidly gyrating as they kept rhythm to the loud syncopated music that filled the night. It was hard not to tap her toes to the beat. Talking was impossible, but it was obvious Bea and Heather were enjoying themselves. She was glad Sophia had talked them into the cruise.

The crowd erupted into catcalls, whistles, and clapping after the show. The dancers walked among the passengers, taking pictures with them while the harbor lights twinkled along the shoreline.

"Come, we will get a picture for you to take home. You will remember the fun time we had tonight."

They all lined up while a photographer snapped their picture with two of the more moderately dressed dancers, and promised them it would be ready for them at the end of the cruise.

"We will go up on deck and relax, take in the night, breathe in what the evening has to offer. Relax." Sophia smiled at the group, took in a deep breath and headed toward the stairs. "But first, I think we will get in line to visit the facilities—it will be another hour before we are back home."

"I'll go up and find a comfortable spot for us. I'll meet you up on deck." Marcia tugged her sweater a little tighter. The air was balmy, tropical, but suddenly a bit cooler.

She found a quiet spot on the top deck in the back of the boat. She leaned over the railing and let the warm tropical breeze play with her hair she had let down for the evening, and tucked it behind her ears. The moon was high above, and the stars reflected and glistened on the calm water. She wrapped her aqua cashmere scarf around her bare shoulders and let the evening moon sparkling on the water mesmerize her thoughts.

Should she call Jared as Sophia suggested? Tell him there was no way she and Brad were getting back together? Would he care? Was it too late? Was he too busy putting his business back together to have time for a relationship? Time for her? Was she ready to face another rejection? Wasn't twice enough? She was better off concentrating on getting her own life back in order—finding a job. She didn't have the finances to wait three months to see if Wild and Wonderful was going to expand. And in Europe or Asia? She didn't want to live with her sister forever. But then, she didn't want to become the family's first bag lady, either.

A young couple, arms entwined, shimmied in next to her. She shifted to the side, giving them space, and nudged up against another couple on the other side. She wondered if there was ever going to be a special someone somewhere out there for her. Or, was she destined to live her life an old spinster? The old-fashioned term made her cringe.

Another young couple slipped in along the railing on the other side of her, oblivious to anything or anyone but themselves. Marcia was shoved closer to the corner, next to the staircase leading down to the stern. As she was about to abandon her spot and search out another location, two men grabbed her arms and dragged her down the stairwell. She reached for the railing, but they snatched her arms in a tight vise-like grip. They yanked them—hard. Her scarf slipped off her shoulders and she tumbled down the stairs, rolled on the slippery surface, and banged her head up against one of the protruding metal structures in the middle of the stern. In a flash, the men covered her entire body with a cold tarp. Dazed from the blow to her head, she lay limp, unable to defend herself. Before she knew what they intended, she was thrown over one of their shoulders and carried away.

"You will not make a noise," one of them

whispered next to her ear loud enough so she understood, even though the tarp covered her head. "You do not want to end up at the bottom of the bay."

She wiggled, hoping they would drop her, but it only caused them to tighten their hold.

"What do you want from me?" she muffled, glad they at least hadn't stuffed something in her mouth, even though no one could hear her at the moment. Music blared around them—so loud even a deaf person could hear it. And those lining the railing were too busy making out with each other to have witnessed her rapid descent to the bottom of the boat. Which meant she was totally on her own.

She was dumped on the floor, the tarp taken away, and her hands yanked behind her back. She looked up to find they had placed her under the overhang of the deck above, where no one could see or hear them. It was darker, but she made out the two men and recognized them as the ones who had attacked her at Christ the Redeemer.

"What do you want?" she asked again.

"It does not matter. Mr. Osaka is still in the market for the prototype that Mr. Rose promised."

"I do not have it."

"Yes, we know. But you do have the connection he needs. He will make an exchange—you for the game. You will contact your brother and get it for us."

"My brother doesn't have the prototype. He isn't Mr. Rose. *Mr. Rose* is in jail."

"It does not matter. Your brother has the connection as well, and will get it in exchange for you."

"And if I don't cooperate?"

"Ah, my dear—" Mr. Osaka stepped through the

side door to confront her. "I am sure Mr. Reed will be more than agreeable to work a deal, do you not agree?"

"No. I don't agree."

There was no way she was going to give in to these thugs.

"We have ways to make you talk. Ask your brother."

The taller of the two grabbed her arm and shoved her up against the wall. He swung his hand toward her face. Marcia shut her eyes and cringed, waiting for the back of his beefy hand to strike. But instead, she heard what sounded like a wild band of screaming Comanche bearing down on them. She opened her eyes to find Sophia and Sammie waving their arms in the air at the two men, yelling and screaming at them to leave her alone. Before the men had a chance to react, the feral women had the men shoved up against the railing, teetering on the edge. Not hesitating, they continued their assault and shoved the men overboard. Stunned, Marcia could only smile at the startled looks on the men's faces as they flipped over the railing. Between the splashes they made when they went overboard, and their yelling and screaming, the passengers on the upper decks crowded the railing to see what the ruckus was all about. The man overboard signal pealed above the music. The music died, and a handful of the crew descended down the stairs in unison. Life rafts were thrown to the sinking men, who were unable to stay afloat due to the ship's wake.

With everyone's attention focused on the commotion taking place in the back of the ship, Marcia sagged against the paneled exterior, relieved it was over. She let out a deep sigh, only to be startled when

Mr. Osaka took advantage of the situation. Gun in hand, he marched her into the boat's dark interior, and shut and locked the door behind him before she had a chance to scream.

Dammit. How had she forgotten about him? Before she could even think about defending herself, he snatched a fist full of her hair and dragged her down the hall. He opened a door on the left and threw her across the room like a rag doll, jarring every bone in her body. Before she could sit up, he had her hands tied behind her back and wrapped a cloth around her mouth. It wouldn't have done her any good to scream at this point—the music up on deck had resumed and no one would hear. She gagged, swallowed, and then forced herself to take slow and steady breaths through her nose. What happened to Bea and Sammie? Would they go for help? Would they find her locked in this room?

"So, there is no one to hear you with all the fuss taking place outside. I will be back when the ship has docked for the night. We will finish this. See if your brother or Mr. Reed cares enough to help save you."

Mr. Osaka opened the door to leave, but his escape was blocked by three crewmembers who sprang into action and knocked the gun out of his hand and wrestled him to the floor. Marsha wanted to clap and shout for joy. However, her hands were tied behind her back and her mouth banded shut.

"I am sorry, Miss Kline." The uniformed official bent to remove the gag from her mouth, and then gently untied her ankles and wrists.

Marcia sucked in air, gulped, and rubbed her aching wrists. She flexed her feet and then made a sad attempt to stand. The officer held her steady until she was able to stand on her own.

"Thank you. How did you know where to find me? That I needed help?"

The ship's officer smiled. "You have a very concerned and convincing sister-in-law. Once she confronted us and told us the whole story, we called ashore to confirm the situation with the police. When we heard the commotion your sister and friend were causing, we mobilized into action. I am sorry to say, despite the men being criminals, they did need saving and have been fished out of the sea. We came down the corridor to avoid the passengers when we saw this man drag you inside. Rest assured, you are safe, now."

"Thank you so much…"

Sammie and Sophia rushed into the room, wrapped their arms around her at the same time, and almost knocked her back off her feet. They held on tight in a big group hug. She appreciated the support and the warm and fuzzy feelings of their arms around her.

"I am so glad to see you two." Marcia scanned the area. "Where is Bea and Heather? Are they okay?"

"They're fine." Sammie brushed her concern aside. "When those two men forced you down the stairs, we sent them to go for help—to tell someone what was going on—why the men were after you. We snuck down the stairs waiting for the right moment to rush them."

"Once more you are safe." Sophia rushed forward and wrapped her arms around her again. "I am so sorry for the trouble you have had to endure here in Rio."

"It's not your fault, Sophia. But they have Mr. Osaka, now. I'm sure it is really all over this time."

"Miss Kline? I am Captain Santos. I have called

the authorities. They assure me these men will be taken care of when we get back to shore. If you will allow me, you and your family can join me on the upper deck where you will be assured a comfortable ride back to the harbor."

"Bea and Heather…"

"Are waiting there for you." The captain smiled, then allowed his assistant to escort them to the bridge.

****

"Jared? I'm glad I caught you. Listen, I need to talk to you about Marcia."

Jared tensed. What the hell was going on down there? What kind of trouble had she gotten into this time?

"What's wrong? What happened to her? Have they caught Osaka? Don't tell me he still thinks she has the damn prototype. *Shit.* I thought everything was taken care of. Now you tell me she's in danger again? Where's her damn fiancé?"

"Calm down. Mr. Holcomb left the same day you did. Marcia stayed behind with her family."

"What? Why didn't you say so? Dammit man, they led me to believe they were getting back together. How the hell can he leave her down there with Osaka on the loose? And you're telling me to calm down?"

"Exactly. If you would calm down and let me tell you…"

"Calm down? Calm down? What the hell. I'm a million miles away, and you call me to say Marcia is in trouble and you want me to calm down? What the hell am I supposed to do back here in Oregon? Have the police been notified?"

"If you'll give me a minute and let me explain. The

police…"

"Get off the damn phone so I can make arrangements to get my jet ready and get down there. Have you called the police? Tried to locate her? Never mind, don't answer. I'm out the door. Have someone pick me up at the airport when I land."

Jared slammed the phone down, picked up his Stetson, and headed out the door. His ranch manager stopped him before he got to the range rover.

"Where are you going in such a hurry, boss? The new hand is having trouble with one of the steers. Thought maybe you could give him a bit of help."

"You're on your own, Cash. You deal with it. In fact, you're totally in charge for the next week. Expect a raise in your next paycheck. I have to head down to Rio. Kurt called. Something's happened to Marcia."

Cash stepped back and grinned.

"Well, now. Don't let me stand in the way of true love. It's about time, Boss. I'll see the ranch runs smooth as a baby's bottom."

"Love? Love has nothing to do with this. The woman is in trouble again, and it's my fault."

"How do you figure?"

"It's Russell's sister, Marcia. If he hadn't been trying to save my hide and my business, and her helping to save his, she wouldn't be in trouble again."

"If you say so." His smile broadened.

"Wipe that stupid grin off your face and get back to work. This isn't a laughing matter."

"If you say so. Give the woman my condolences."

"What the hell are you talking about? Condolences for what? Don't tell me her brother didn't make it. God almighty."

"No. I'm sure Russell is doing just fine. Having to put up with you in this frame of mind is what I'm talking about. Have a nice flight."

Jared glared a warning at his ranch hand. The man didn't know what the hell he was talking about. He waved him aside and headed straight for his vehicle—and his jet.

****

Marcia's mind buzzed with the recent incident on the dinner cruise as she lay in bed. With the shock of being hog-tied and used as a bartering tool for Jared's avatar prototype, it had been heartwarming watching Sammie and Sophia rush into action like a SWAT team. She smiled to think they cared enough to put their lives on the line to save her butt.

She drew the lightweight cover-up over her shoulders, shook her head to dispel the sadness that filled her soul. Thoughts of what Osaka had had in store for her. She shut her eyes, blinking back the shudder that washed over her tired body. After what they had done to Russell—beaten him and left him for dead—it was obvious Osaka had intended the same fate befall her had she not been rescued. She owed her sister and Sophia, as well as Bea, a lifetime of gratitude.

It was time to rethink her future, not that she still had one. Right now, she'd ship out to any port Wild and Wonderful had to offer as long as it was as far away from Rio de Janeiro and Jared Reed as possible.

Marcia sniffed, pounded the pillow, rolled over, and stared out the window into a cloudless starry night. She never felt more lonely than she did at that moment.

Alone and broken hearted.

Chapter Sixteen

"I can't leave your side for a second without you getting in trouble." Jared stormed out onto the patio, stopping in front of Marcia.

"*Jared*! What are you doing here? I thought you went back to Oregon?" Marcia sprang to her feet, her coffee lapping over the rim of the mug she held in her hand. With shaking fingers, she set it on the glass table.

"It's about time." Kurt stood, slapped Jared on the shoulder, then stepped aside, a satisfied expression on his devilish face.

"I knew you would come." Sophia clapped her hands together and brought them to her ample chest. "Oh, my. It did not take you so long. But, Jared, you should have been there. What a splash we all made."

"I'm not so happy about your part in it, my dear," Kurt told his wife, an indulgent smile meant for her alone, his eyes trained on her. "But I'm glad you were there to help defuse the situation."

"I'm glad you were there, too." Jared kept his eyes on Marcia. "What the hell happened?"

Her eyebrows rose. What could she say? Tongue-tied, she stammered, only to be interrupted.

"I tried to tell you on the phone, but you wouldn't listen to a word I said. You panicked and hung up on me." Kurt's lips twisted into a humorous grin.

"Well, I'm here now. Fill me in. I'm listening."

Before Marcia could utter a word, Sophia and Sammie started talking at the same time.

"Oh, Jared. It was like a television episode on *The Love Boat* show. The *capitão* showed up and arrested that Osaka crook who wanted to steal your game tape," Sophia sputtered, her hands flying about, her animated face comical.

"He was about to kidnap Marcia to exchange her for the prototype. Sophia and I rushed in and tossed the two men overboard. They deserved it, I can tell you. Then the alarm for 'man overboard' started wailing overhead, and all hell broke loose. What a show." Sammie's voice carried above the others, adding to the confusion.

"Wait a minute." Jared swung his gaze to the others surrounding him.

Marcia wanted them all to leave. She wanted to know why Jared had flown back to Rio and had rushed in all upset with her, when he'd only left two days ago. And she didn't want an audience when he finally said the words she was longing to hear. Hoping to hear.

"You are all confusing me," Jared continued. "None of this makes any sense. Maybe you should let Marcia explain what happened?"

"I'm fine, by the way." Marcia wrung her hands. He hadn't asked. Did he even care? But then if he didn't, what was he doing here?

She took a deep breath. "It's like Sophia and Sammie said, the men must have followed us onboard the dinner cruise and waited until I was alone up on desk. It was crowded. I was enjoying the evening when two men grabbed me and shoved me down the stairs in the back of the boat. I fell down the last few steps, lost my balance, and rolled up against one of the metal fittings on the stern. They threw a tarp over me and hid me under the upper deck's overhang. Mr. Osaka appeared. He demanded I contact Russell. They planned to use me to extort the prototype from him...you. He dragged me into a room and intended to leave me there until after the dinner cruise was over and everyone left. But several crew members arrived in a rush, tackled and restrained him. Then the captain showed up and arrested him." She drew in a deep breath. "Thankfully, Bea had informed the captain about the incident, and the background information behind the whole sordid affair."

"I hope to God they are either dead or behind bars." Jared reached for her. Marcia didn't hesitate. She was in his arms in a heartbeat.

"Behind bars," the three women said all at once.

"I think this is the part where we go find something else to do this evening." Kurt took Sophia's hand in his and tugged her from her chair. He slipped his arm around her waist and led her toward the glass sliding door. "You women might want to take your coffee into the kitchen, as well," he called over his shoulder.

"As much as I'd love to stay and witness this magic moment,"—Sammie stood and beamed at the two of them—"I think I need to help Bea get Heather settled for the night. Right, Bea?"

"Yes. Yes. Of course," Bea mumbled.

"But I'm not tired." Heather leaned back in her chair.

"You don't have to be tired. We need to leave these two lovebirds alone so they can patch things up. Come on. How about a game of rummy?"

"Oh. Oh, yes. Sorry." Heather hopped up from her chair and rushed ahead of her mother. "Can I deal first?"

Marcia's eyes remained glued to Jared as everyone filed out around them, leaving them alone on the patio so they could have a bit of privacy. They didn't need to witness her making a spectacle of herself over Jared a second time.

The temperate evening breeze held a hint of fragrance from Sophia's gardens. Marcia inhaled deeply, hoping to calm her jumbled nerves. And build up the gumption to tell Jared how pleased she was to see him. She let out her tightly held breath. He finally took her hands and wrapped them gently in his own. His touch drew her forward. He tugged her close—their lips met for a long, heart-stopping moment. When he released her, she didn't want to let go. She wrapped her arms around his neck and leaned into him.

"I know a secluded lagoon where we can be alone and finish where we left off the other night." Jared wiggled his eyebrows, nuzzled her neck, and rubbed his hands along her spine and then settled them on her hips.

Marcia's face flamed—partially with embarrassment over what had happened on the beach, and then afterwards—the words they had exchanged, and partly because of the words he'd just uttered—implying he wanted to resume their love-making, with the promise of them forging a relationship. Was a happy-ever-after more important to her than whatever Jared was about to offer? His serious-looking stare confused her. It didn't matter what he wanted. She was tired of searching for love in all the wrong men. She was going to accept whatever he was willing to offer without reservation. She loved him—had loved him for the past two years. There was no way to escape those strong feelings.

"I'm so sorry I deserted you at the airport when I left," he whispered, then kissed her neck, and rubbed his hands seductively up and down her back.

His touch sent slivers of electrical sparks shooting to her inner core. She wished he'd stop talking.

"I am such a heel. But in my own defense, at the time I thought you and Holcomb were still an item. That you were going to resume your vows. The only thing I could do was bow out. What I really wanted to do was punch his lights out. You two aren't an item, are you? Am I making a fool of myself again?"

"I'm glad you didn't attack Brad. But, no, Jared, Brad and I are not an item. I'm sorry if I led you to believe we were. The only excuse I have is that my pride got the best of me. I didn't think you really cared." She snuggled into his warm and inviting embrace, tucked her head in the crux of his neck and sighed. "It was over between me and Brad when I walked in his office and found him with my aerobics instructor. Brad wasn't an easy man to convince that we were no longer engaged."

He rubbed his hands along her arms and then put space between them while he held her gaze.

"I was on my way back to apologize, to see if you would give me one more shot. But I saw the two of you wrapped in each other's arms. I thought the worst—that I left it too late. So I took my wounded ego and high-tailed it back to the ranch. Even my ranch manager thought I was a blockhead."

"Oh, Jared. What you happened to witness was

Brad trying to convince me to stay. If you'd stuck around another minute, you would have seen him leave—without me."

"Oh, Marcia. I'm so sorry I put us through this. And to think I assumed Holcomb was here to protect you—I never would have left you alone if I'd known."

He tightened his hold, his hip leaned into hers suggestively. Weak-kneed, she hung on for support, loving every inch of the contact. He kissed her forehead.

"Shall we take a walk in the garden where we'll have a bit more privacy?"

He snatched her up into a loving embrace. Marcia's breath caught and was taken away when Jared kissed her like there was no tomorrow. She gave as good as she got, her arms twining around his neck. She couldn't get close enough. His kiss turned slow, tender, sending a razor-sharp need coursing through every inch of her being. She leaned her head into his chest, resting there in order to catch her breath.

"I'd rather find that secluded beach…"

"You got it," he rasped. "I'm sure no one here will miss us."

An hour later, after making love on the moonlit beach, they strolled hand in hand in the wake of the waves lapping the sandy shoreline.

"I'm such a fool for having wasted the last two years knowing I almost lost you."

"Let's face it, you had too many things on your mind at the time and no time for a relationship. It would have been a disaster then. Now…"

"Now, I don't know what I'd do without you. Will you marry me?"

Epilogue

The early morning mist was heavy as Marcia's and Jared's family gathered around Christ the Redeemer on Corcovado Mountain. Russell stood next to Bea and Heather, with the aid of crutches, and Sammie and Sophia stood beside Marcia.

"Relax. Stop twisting that poor bouquet—you're going to have those beautiful rose petals scattered all over the place before you get a chance to say 'I do.' He'll be here," Sammie whispered. "He wouldn't have hopped his jet as fast as he did to come down to make sure you were safe if he didn't love you."

"He's late. What if he changed his mind?"

"Traffic, I'm sure. He's not changing his mind."

"What if he did? You know my track record—it's not so great. I'm a liability he doesn't need."

"Stop it. He'll be here."

A hand rested on Marcia's shoulder, sending a familiar warmth deep inside. She sighed. He made it after all.

"I'm right here." Jared leaned in and placed a soft kiss on her neck below her ear.

Marcia's legs grew weak, her eyes closed, her insides melted—had her dreams really come true? She sighed. She was finally going to get married to the man she loved. A man who truly loved her. Jared wasn't letting her down. He'd come back for her, and she couldn't be any giddier than a schoolgirl on her first date. She leaned into him. He gathered her in his arms and held on tight.

"You ready to do this?"

She looked up into his sexy, smiling eyes—the certainty of his love shone down on her, his smile wide and confident.

"Absolutely. I love you."

Jared kissed her nose. "I love you too."

He addressed the officiating priest with a nod. The priest returned the nod, smiled, and began the ceremony. Everyone gathered close, not wanting to miss a word. The mist rose into the clear azure sky and swirled around and then up off the monolithic statue of Christ the Redeemer's outstretched arms as if to bless the marriage.

Marcia thought it a very good omen indeed when the sun shone down on the hillside and Jared kissed her as soon as they were pronounced man and wife.

"Are you ready?" He wiggled his eyebrows and gave her that crooked grin she had come to love.

The gleam in Jared's eyes was a bit puzzling. "What do you have in mind?"

"I've arranged a special surprise. I hope you like it. Trust me?"

The only other time he'd asked her that, they'd been sliding down a cable.

"Jared?"

"Come on. Let's say goodbye to the family."

They received well wishes and congratulations as they made their way toward the steps, their hands clasped firmly together. Marcia was taken aback when Sammie handed her a change of clothes.

"What are these for?"

"I don't think you want to hang glide down off this mountain in that dress."

"What? Jared?"

He swung her up into his arms and kissed the concerned frown off her face.

"My wedding present to you. What better way to start the rest of our lives together than by hanging on and trusting each other to make it over the long haul. I'll be right there by your side—always."

A word about the author...

Carol Henry is an author of Destination: Romance—Exotic Romantic Suspense Adventures, as well as contemporary romance and historic women's fiction. She is an international traveler and travel writer of exotic locations for major cruise lines' deluxe in-cabin books. Carol lives with her husband in the beautiful New York State Finger Lakes region where they are surrounded by family and friends.

Find her at:

www.carolhenry.org

~*~

Other Carol Henry titles
available from The Wild Rose Press, Inc.:

AMAZON CONNECTION
SHANGHAI CONNECTION
NOTHING SHORT OF A MIRACLE
RIBBONS OF STEEL